TEI

New Short Stories

Edited by Courttia Newland

Assistant Editor: Nii Ayikwei Parkes

A Tell Tales Paperback

Tell Tales Volume I
Editor: Courttia Newland

First published in the United Kingdom 2004.

ISBN: 0-9547761-0-0

Acknowledgements

Tell Tales is grateful to The Arts Council of England for its financial assistance.

Heartfelt thanks also to Shilland, Borders, the BBC Roots initiative, and our many regional partners including the Save Our Short Story Campaign for their support.

The Tell Tales Trio: Marrianne San Miguel, Courttia Newland and Nii Ayikwei Parkes.

"live to tell the tale; tell the tale to live"

Are we sitting comfortably?

They say that there are 8 million stories in the big city. We couldn't gather them all, so here are 15. These stories cover hopes and fears, love and loss, laughter and speculation, without ever losing sight of their main purpose – to tell a tale.

In the city, storytelling is how we writers communicate our thoughts on the world around us. We breath in the smells, fumes and atmosphere, then breath out imaginary places and characters, parallel worlds and doppelgangers of what we inhale every day. Sometimes we kid ourselves that it's all for our own self-expression. At other times we admit that we also do it for the enjoyment of those who simply live, to see their bright smiles of recognition. We tell tales for all of the above reasons, and yet for none. We tell the tales in order to survive. We tell the tales because they have always been told.

Courttia Newland

West London 2004

CONTENTS

X Men Reject

Sharon Jennings

So what's wrong with me then? I should have at least been asked to come back for a recall, or interview or something. I stayed up all night thinking about this and why they didn't want me in their group. More like in the old days, those country clubs that excluded blacks or something. But to be fair I couldn't say that it was a colour thing because they did have some brothers and sisters in there already and in fact, so many of them were so many different colours I guess that didn't really matter. Besides it's 2204 and Earth stopped that kind of thing long time ago. Now if it's Mars we're talking about, that's another thing. Now they are a bunch of bigots.

No it must have been something else. But what? I showed them my best work, my best looks, stares, stance. My locks were flowing, wiggling, twisting, hissing, ready for anything. I showed 'em and they still said no. They said I would be a risk. That I needed to get in close in order to strike and I had no particular strength or power to enable me to get in that close. So it all depended on luck or the stupidity of the other person.

I really don't see why that was so important anyway. That's what the rest of them are for, isn't it? To cover my back? Shit, I even had a name and everything. I had gone through a few, you know, like Snake Woman, Reptilia, that kind of thing. But in the end,

I settled on Medusa. Actually the name had been given to me. By Gambit. One night when, well let's just say he played all the aces that night. Cherie! Uhh Ma Petite!

Anyway, it was him that told me about the vacancy and suggested I tried out. You see Storm had decided she was tired of storming and wanted to give up the fast life. She had met this guy with some minor power, I think he could make rain or something and she thought the two of them could make a go of it, maybe even have some kids, so she quit.

When I got to the tryouts, there were all these uh, people, everywhere and I kinda thought I was out of my league. There was this kind of committee at the front, headed by Professor X, of course. His bald head gleaming, squint black eyes, and a voice that made you want to run to your Mama. But I fronted it out and when it was my turn, he actually smiled at me and asked me to step up to the front of the room and introduce myself and then, demonstrate my power. Well I couldn't really demonstrate on anybody there so I brought along my own volunteer, a rabbit. Someone had written that being near to live animals helped the body produce melanin, and you know we need as much as we can get now that the Ozone layer is gone. So I bought this little rabbit and fed him up but I was never a lover of pets and just waited until the day I could think of putting him to good use. And here it was.

Oh, haven't I told you my power? I can turn people to stone. Yeah me, Medusa!

I discovered I had this power by pure accident five years ago when I was 16. I had got to the age when I wanted to stop taking the hair straightening tablets. You know I had read so much about the harm that those chemicals could do, anyway I wanted to be more singular.

So many of us, I mean Africanoids are so confused about who we are and what we should look like. The Media doesn't help either. Images of blue skin and purple eyes, it's the multi-hued look that's in. Since the re-unification of races after World War 6, the world governments agreed that everyone (on Earth anyway) should be made up of all the remaining races, or what was left of them after the massive amounts of radiation the human race soaked up. People literally became colours over night, black and white were replaced with blue and green or any other colour you could imagine. That was about the time they started discovering that some people had powers, mutants they called them.

Most people just mixed naturally and soon you got all these different colour combinations. But us? Our people didn't want to trust natural. You know, we spend some serious money to get that designer, vari-colour look. You know how we stay. But me, I just wanted to get away from all that and just look uni-racial. Trouble was, my hair was so used to being chemicalised that it went through some serious withdrawal and all fell out. That lasted 24 hours. After that it started growing again. And I tell you. I never seen anything like it before. It was all coarse and tight like little beads, and it kept growing and fusing into this mass of, I don't know. And it just kept on coming. It got springy, and woolly, covering my whole head. I couldn't get any of the Power Combs to go through it so it developed these dips and bumps all over.

In my History class we watched a tele-vid which showed people with hair like mine. They called it Afro after the land of Afro, where we all supposedly originated. That continent no longer exists, hasn't done for about 150 years but that was way before my time and frankly I find history so boring.

Anyway, in that same History class, we also saw people wearing something called Dreadlocks, which I think are the forerunners of our Solar Locks – or Solars. They're called that because people who wear them have to have extract of sunlight injections to make their hair grow. Apparently in the old days people just twisted their hair up and then the 'locks' just grew. I decided that I would try it, the old-fashioned way. Just twist up my hair.

At first it didn't work, the twists just got all tangled up. But I kept trying, twisting them smaller and tighter, keeping my head wrapped in cloth day and night to protect them, and oiling them with natural sebum that we can extract directly from our glands, to prevent dehydration.

3 months later, I had the beginnings of the Solars. It was then that I started talking to them, cooing and coaxing them, even playing them music and letting them free to

blow in the breeze at sunset. Every weekend I took my Solars to the coast so that they could roll and dance in the sea air. They loved this. I knew because every time my whole scalp would tingle as if they were trying to say thank you.

So in about 6 months my Solars were shoulder length, black, shiny and strong. They gleamed in the sun and hummed whenever they got wet.

One day, getting ready for school, I decided to wear my hair unwrapped so that everybody of could see how long my Solars had got. But as soon as I got into my first lesson there was trouble. The teacher, Mr Adams who never did like me, told me that my hair was too long and untidy to be worn to school like that. He told me to tie it up, or cut it, he didn't care, he just wanted me out of his class until I had done something about it.

That bastard! Who did he think he was?! I remember getting so mad that I couldn't move. I just stood there staring back at him and for a second, just one second I wished the fucker would drop dead. Just as I thought this, I felt a heavy, jolt of electricity shoot through me and my head, my head, felt like it was on fire. I thought my head was going to split in two. That was the last thing I remembered.

I woke up in Miss Burns office. She was the Vice Principal for girls. She was straight on the vidie-phone to my mother saying she had to come and take me from the school now. She didn't speak to me and wouldn't look at me. This was strange because she normally stared girls into submission.

I asked her what had happened. What had I done? She didn't say anything, but when my mom got there, I overheard Miss Burns telling her everything.

Apparently, the man turned to stone. And it was my hair that did it. My hair, my lovely Solars had turned to snakes, black shiny snakes. Hissing and spitting. Mr Adams was shouting at me to get out of his class one minute, frozen solid the next.

Well , since then I've developed a little more control. I don't have to be angry, but it helps. Works quicker that way. And I don't pass out every time I 'stone' somebody. But I have to look at the person and they have to look at me. And that's what Professor X said made me a liability.

I still don't think it's fair. I would make a good X-men female: Rogue, Jubilee, Jean Grey, oh she is a real bitch, and Medusa! Besides, since Storm left they need another Sister.

The Boy Who Stole The Ocean

Rajeev Balasubramanyam

Somu was eleven when his sister died but for twelve months he refused to cry. The police said it was an accident, but Somu was there. He saw it.

It was bonfire night. A group of boys splashed petrol from the barbecue over Parvati's salvar kameez, then threw lighted matches at her. It was supposed to be a game, but it took her two days to die, her lifeless eyes staring at him from the hospital bed. When she caught fire the adults rushed around looking for water. But there wasn't any water.

Weeks later, every day after school, Somu could be found at the edge of the pier, staring into the ocean. He would sit there till dark, come home, eat his dinner, and go to bed.

'Why does he spend all his time by the ocean?' said his father after Somu was asleep.

'He needs to heal in his own way,' his mother replied.

'But the boy should cry,' said his father. 'I've never seen him cry.'

'He'll cry when he's ready,' said Somu's mother.

But months passed and Somu's eyes remained dry. Then, on a cold afternoon in

April, Somu started into the sea and saw a face staring back at him. It was her, Parvarti, his beloved elder sister, shimmering inside the water. She looked neither solid nor transparent, but something in between. She wasn't smiling or frowning; she was simply there, looking at him.

Somu was so astonished he didn't leave the pier until long after dark.

In the months afterward, Somu visited his sister every day. He would talk to her, though she never moved or replied, and sometimes he brought her gifts; the petals of flowers or sweets his mother had made. He would throw them at the water and, as they broke the surface, Parvati's image would quiver in gratitude.

His parents noticed the change in him.

'It must be the ocean,' his mother said. 'I told you it was good for him.'

'But he still hasn't cried,' his father warned.

'We don't know that. Who knows what he does when he's by himself.'

'I know,' said his father. 'I know my boy.'

When the summer ended and the days became longer, a factory appeared by the entrance to the pier. There used to be a hotel there, but they had knocked it down. The process was noisy. Somu endured it, knowing it would end.

When the factory was up and running, they constructed an aluminium pipe that led to the water's edge, very near to Somu's favourite spot. One Saturday in October, Somu watched as an ugly green fluid emerged from the pipe and entered the ocean. As the days went by, more and more of this fluid appeared until the water turned green. It became hard for Somu to see his sister face, and he knew she would troubled by it. It made him angry, but there was nothing he could do.

The following Friday, Somu's father came home in an anxious mood. He found Somu in his bedroom, sat beside him, and put an arm around his shoulders.

'Somu,' his father said, 'I don't know how to tell you this, but somebody stole the ocean. I'm sorry, son; I know how much it meant to you.'

'But, Dad,' said Somu. 'That's impossible. You can't steal the ocean.'

'Go see for yourself, son,' his father replied.

Somu rushed to the pier and looked out. It was true. The ocean had gone. Where there used to be water as far as the eye could see, there was now a huge cavity, as dry as the desert. And Parvati was nowhere to be seen.

Somu grinned. And then laughed, a greedy, triumphant laugh.

It was he who had stolen it, late last night. He had sneaked out of the house, clambered to the shore, and drunk the entire ocean. Now it was in his stomach, and it would stay there. Parvati would be safe, and no-one would turn the water green.

It was the following morning that Parvati began to talk to Somu. He thought it was his stomach rumbling at first, but then he realised it was her. Her voice sounded strange, a little like whale song, but the words were clear enough.

'Somu,' she said, 'it was a very brave thing that you did, but you have to put me back. We can't stay here, the ocean and I. We need to be outdoors.'

'But, Parvati,' Somu protested. 'Didn't you see what they were doing? It's better like this, I promise you...'

'No, Somu,' said Parvati. 'You put us back. This isn't right.'

'I don't care,' said Somu, shaking his head. 'I won't do it.'

'You do it,' said Parvati, 'or else'.

'Or else what?' answered Somu. 'What are you going to do?'

The fight lasted for hours. In spite of everything, Somu was delighted. It was good to be arguing with his sister again.

During dinner Somu tried to keep silent, but his sister kept taunting him. 'Silly little twerp,' she would say. 'Put me back, you moron.'

Somu couldn't take it anymore.

'No!' he yelled, which made his parents stare at him in astonishment: had he finally lost his mind?

'Excuse me,' said Somu, leaving the table. 'I need to go for a walk.'

'Son, what's the matter?" His father called after him. 'Whatever it is, we can talk about it.'

'Let him go,' said Somu's mother. 'This can't be easy for him.'

Somu ran outside, across the beach, and into the desert where the ocean used to be. The police had cordoned off the area and he was free to make as much noise as he liked.

'No way!' he yelled. 'I'm not putting you back, and that's it.'

'Somu,' said his sister. 'Don't be silly now. You have to. The fishermen have nowhere to fish, the birds are hungry, and it doesn't rain anymore. You have to put us back.'

'Sorry, Parvati,' said Somu, 'but I won't do it. I've made up my mind, you'll see.'

'No, you'll see,' said his sister, suddenly angry again. 'I'm three years older than you, you insect, you see what I do to you.'

'You can't do anything to me,' said Somu. 'You're dead.'

There was a terrible silence. Somu hadn't meant to say that. He knew he had hurt his sister's feelings.

'That's true,' said Parvati, at last. 'I am dead. I can't deny it, and really, I don't mind. I'm at peace now. But what you, Somu? You're alive, aren't you? I've been watching you since I died, you, and you went to school every day, and you did all your schoolwork and you ate all your meals and you went to sleep at night, but you never cried. Why didn't you cry?'

'I'm sorry,' said Somu, his voice shaking. 'I don't know why. I should have, I suppose.'

'It's never too late,' said Parvati. 'You ought to cry; you'll feel better.'

'I don't want to,' said Somu, with tears in his eyes. 'It isn't fair.'

'Nothing is fair, Somu,' his sister answered. 'That isn't the point. You have to cry. You have to feel better.'

Too tired to argue anymore, Somu lay on his back and closed his eyes.

Before he knew it, like the sudden approach of a storm, he began to cry. His sobs grew and grew until he was weeping freely, huge teardrops falling from his eyes and onto his nose, splashing onto the ground. He cried all night without a pause, and in the morning he fell asleep, the most comfortable sleep of his life.

When Somu awoke he was floating in the ocean. He looked around him and, about a mile away, he saw the pier and the grey outline of the factory. Very gently, the waves brought him to the shore, where he climbed to his feet and looked out across the water.

His sister was smiling at him, her reflection glistening in the morning sun. Somu smiled back and waved goodbye, before turning to leave. He felt much lighter as he walked home, as if all his pain and sadness had drained away with his tears.

This Is Not A Love Story

Liam Gallimore-Wells

Shopping could be viewed as a kind of performing art because something dramatic usually happens when I see Bella at the local supermarket. Bella came from Bristol and worked as a checkout girl there. She was Bengali and beautiful and had the best-looking body I'd ever seen. Bella bore a striking resemblance to a girl I fell in love with. One day the girl called round and gave me an ultimatum: either I quit drooling over Bella or we were finished. We loved each other and all that, but deep down I knew it was over. I was hooked on Bella and she knew it.

This supermarket where Bella worked was unique because all the men inside never bought anything. Bella's pretty form affected them all in different ways, but everyone liked her because the sight of her well-shaped breasts brought a special sense of drama to the routine of a busy supermarket. So there I was, back in this supermarket on a Saturday keeping my eyes peeled for Bella, when I bumped into Beresford, a Barbadian bus driver from Bayswater. Beresford was browsing through different brands of brown bread when I asked him if he'd seen Bella about.

'Over on checkout ten, brother!' He said, beaming.

So I started walking to checkout ten, eyes still peeled for Bella. I was almost there when I bumped into Benny, a Brazilian bartender from Bethnal Green. Benny was busy buying basmati when I asked him if he'd seen Bella.

But he didn't hear what I said because he was too busy gawping at her.

Bella was standing on checkout ten and looking as glamorous as usual when I finally clapped eyes on her. Tonight Bella was being filmed by a crew of cameramen for a successful new docu-drama about the trials and tribulations of being Bengali and beautiful in a busy urban supermarket. You could tell Bella was getting carried away by all the attention. She clearly enjoyed playing to the cameras as they shadowed her movements, pouting her mouth and fluttering her eyelids provocatively. As she moved about, I sensed Bella had a profound need in her to exaggerate her beauty. So much so that one of the cameramen only just narrowly avoided walking straight into a pillar as he trundled behind her, filming her hips swaying capriciously as she walked round the cash register.

I was having a good long ogle myself when I bumped into Byron, a burly Zimbabwean barrister from Brixton. So I asked him what he thought of Bella.

'Not my type bro. Anyway I don't like girls from Bristol,' he mumbled, with one eye rooted to Bella's bristols bobbing up and down in youthful unison.

There was no denying. Bella was beautiful, with a body made in heaven. She was a born star. But sometimes the stars make us cry and watching Bella being filmed on the boards of this busy supermarket wasn't really helping. I realized Bella's beauty might stand the test of time as she was being captured on celluloid, and this thought sent powerful new pictures of her seductive form hurtling through my head. For a moment standing there, my whole mind felt like a giant electronic screen shimmering with her immaculate image.

But enough as enough. I turned away and headed off down the aisle of the frozen meat section, frowning.

Bella was beginning to get the better of me.

Since the girl I loved told me we were finished, I'd become like all the other men in the supermarket, all shadows of our former selves who went shopping when they didn't need to in this dull urban supermarket to drool over a checkout girl. Bella was close to becoming an indelible icon in the archives of our minds, so I resolved to confront this problem, and then try to win back the affections of the girl I loved. It wouldn't be easy, but I made up my mind and there was no going back.

I had this sleek silver .22 semi automatic which I always kept at home in a glass case under the couch, but tonight it was in my right hand in the side pocket of my duffel coat. The barrel was loaded and the smooth handle felt cold and dangerous in my hand.

I knew Bella would still be on checkout ten.

My arms were tingling and I felt nervous as I turned and headed back past the frozen chicken breasts and lamb chops. Everything around me seemed to move in slow motion and I could hear the blood pumping through my veins, getting faster and faster. It seemed to take ages to even blink when I looked up in the middle of the frozen meat section and saw a sign that read:

MIDDLE OF THE FROZEN MEAT SECTION

I was about to take centre stage on the boards of this busy supermarket and gatecrash Bella's new TV drama with a one-off cameo role destined to rock the airwaves and transform this everyday supermarket saga into cutting-edge viewing. I figured I might look more inconspicuous if I actually bought something this time, so I picked up a leg of lamb and tucked it under my left arm on my way to Bella's checkout.

Bella was still surrounded by cameramen as I joined the queue.

I tried to stay calm because I knew this was my big chance to expose Bella's beauty in a new light and put an end to this thing for good. I wondered what might happen if something went wrong and I played this thought back inside my head like a nerve-jangling clip from a silent movie.

But it was time to make a stand.

Bella was standing up on the checkout now with her back to me. So I clenched the gun firmly in my hand and took aim. My arm was outstretched and everything was going to script until I felt someone tap me on the shoulder from behind.

I was gobsmacked and couldn't believe my eyes when I quickly glanced round with my arm still outstretched to see the girl I loved standing there right beside me in the queue, smiling.

I smiled back in disbelief and my pulse was racing when I turned back towards Bella and fired.

Bella jolted violently and collapsed into the cash register and onto the floor, sending a crate of mangos tumbling off the checkout conveyor belt.

The mangos made a soft thudding sound as they hit the ground and Bella was out of sight when a brutal cracking noise filled the air like a terrifying new sound effect. The mangos hurtled away across the floor like delinquents fleeing a break-in as a tall, crane-like camera swung round over my head, zooming in to shoot a close-up on Bella.

She was sprawled in a motionless heap on the floor with a bullet-sized hole in her forehead and swathes of dark hair flung randomly across her face. She looked desperately alone as her eyes stared vacantly up into the camera with a thick line of blood oozing from her mouth and down into a small scarlet puddle on the floor. All I could hear now was silence and this silence was very loud as I stared down at Bella.

I'd finally got my big break on the boards of this extraordinary supermarket and I turned round to hold the girl I loved in my arms again. But instead all I saw was a grey-haired old man with a stick. He was cowering away from me and looked afraid.

The last thing I remember is watching Bella slowly rise to her feet as the director frantically waved his hands in the air shouting: 'Cut - OK people, let's run that one more time!'

Going Under

Matt Thorne

'We could always sell my flute.'

He rolled over on the bed and hugged her. They always had this conversation on Sunday afternoons. Although the amount of money he needed to get by was fairly fluid, Anya had weekly expenses that had to be met. Most important was her Oyster card, topped up with twenty pounds every Monday. When their funds were low (usually the third week of each month, when the financial tide had gone out and wouldn't return until the beginning of the next), they got desperate and argued, then made up and sought out solutions.

Paul was used to this. His father, a compulsive gambler, was often in need of ready cash. There were two occasions that stayed with him. The first was when they were on holiday in Spain and his dad had persuaded his mum to go with him to a Casino. They'd abandoned Paul and his brother in front of an inappropriate cabaret that was little more than a glorified strip show and disappeared off to play roulette. By midnight his father had lost all the money he'd brought for the family holiday and there was still nine days left. At six a.m. the following morning he was out by the swimming pool, attempting to sell not only his watch and all the clothes from the family's suitcases, but also the furniture from their hotel room. The only lucky break he got that whole holiday was that he wasn't arrested.

The second occasion Paul remembered came at the end of a spectacularly bad run of poor fortune for his father. After nursing Paul's grandfather through a grisly series of cancer treatments (he got so high on morphine that he started hallucinating that the hospital trolleys moving through the corridors were trains dropping off unpleasant creatures from another dimension who were coming to get him), he was playing on a service station fruit machine on the way up to see him when the old man finally died. In his will, Paul's grandfather left all his assets to Paul's father. He didn't have much, but he did own his house, a two-bedroom terrace in an OK neighbourhood. The house had been valued at about twenty thousand pounds, but although it was structurally sound, towards the end Paul's grandfather had let it fall into a state of disrepair. Paul's father believed that if he did some work on it he could boost the property's value by at least five thousand pounds. This turned out to be true. He worked on the house for three months and sold it for just over twenty-five thousand.

He lost the whole amount a week later, in one night of poker. It was the kind of game at which Paul's father would never normally have been able to buy a seat at the table. His inexperience cost him. Gamblers rarely have much in the way of assets and it wasn't long before he had to sell the only other thing of value Paul's grandfather had left him. Paul's grandfather had smoked since he was eleven, and from the moment he bought his first packet of cigarettes he had swapped brands according to whoever was producing the most interesting cigarette cards. Over the years he amassed an incredible collection, sending away for the limited edition albums that accompanied each series. It had been a hobby for him, and he'd never given any thought to the possibility that the collection might have anything other than sentimental value.

If Paul's father had been sensible, with careful research, he could have slowly sold the collection off in sections to the highest bidder, making almost as much as he'd got from the house. Instead, one desperate Sunday he found a want ad in one of the antiques magazines he bought every Saturday even though he'd never owned an antique in his life. He called up the number and told the man on the other end of the line to come round with as much cash as he could rustle up.

The man arrived an hour later. His excitement was obvious. His fingers were trembling as he turned the pages of each catalogue. Peter knew his father was making a terrible mistake. Although he couldn't control his body, the man kept up the normal purchaser's patter, pointing out miniscule creases on the cards and tutting at misplaced hinges. The man offered seven hundred pounds for the complete collection. Paul's father, thinking he was being clever, demanded a thousand. The man went outside and got the balance from his wife, who was sitting in the car outside their house. Feeling guilty, aware he'd done something stupid, Paul's father had tried to make it up to Paul by taking him and his brother to the cinema that afternoon. Watching the film, Paul realised that when his father died he would leave him nothing except memories of the occasional good times, but he loved him and felt grateful for these two hours together: a temporary relief from the normal grind of their day-to-day existence.

Usually, Paul wouldn't even consider the possibility of Anya selling her flute. But, today, because they were desperate, he asked, 'How much do you think it'd be worth?'

'It's a really good flute, y'know. I think my parents paid a thousand for it.'

'Really?' he said. 'And do those sort of things hold their value?'

'Well,' she said tentatively, 'we could get at least seven hundred for it.'

'Who from?'

'We'd put an advert in Loot. Someone would want it.'

The amount of money the flute was worth reminded him of his father, almost putting him off the idea. He remember a later time when his father had come to his bedroom and begged him to let him sell the video camera Paul had won in a school competition. Anya could tell he was wavering and said, 'Look, I never play it any more.'

He smiled. 'Play it for me.'

'What?'

'One last time. Then we'll sell it.'

She found some sheet music and played an Erik Satie composition. She was so beautiful when she played it made him cry. He didn't know what it was that affected him so much: the way she concentrated, or moved her head, or feet. He wanted to tell her they didn't have to sell it, but he knew they did. There was no one else they could borrow money from; no way he could get together even the smallest amount of cash. So they put an ad in the paper and three days later a red-headed woman came round. She was a serious type, with glasses and a stern mouth. Paul was glad the flute was going to this woman, but cross when she tried to haggle about the price. He told her, 'My girlfriend's really sad she has to sell it. But we really need the money.'

The woman pursed her lips. 'I'm not sure it's worth seven hundred pounds.'

'You know it is,' he said. 'Please, this is a really emotional moment for me.'

She gave him the money and left the flat, clearly cross with herself. Paul called Anya at work and told her he had sold the flute; they didn't have to worry for another fortnight. Anya didn't seem worried about who had bought her instrument, and wasn't at all emotional about the loss. He loved her for this.

They went out for dinner that night. They were careful, but they still managed to spend more than they intended. That was the problem with being so close to running out altogether: it was so stressful that every time they got a break they'd relax and put themselves back in the position they'd only just escaped. But what was the point of living if you didn't allow yourself a small treat every now and again? Things would be different when they had children, he knew that. He supposed it was like gambling. This realisation came as shock to him. He wondered whether it was an inherited gene that made him act this way.

Although Paul always thought of his grandfather as a saintly man, the truth was he had been an alcoholic. Paul's father thought he had conquered his genetic inheritance, yet the gambling was simply a replacement addiction. Was being a spendthrift a similar psychological weakness? It wasn't that he didn't try: he did everything he could to boost his cash-flow, and struggled harder than almost anyone he knew. But he knew those a lot worse off than him and they seemed to get by.

What was his sin? Living beyond his means? No, it was more than that. It was refusing to accept all those things that normal people went through to structure their life. Finding a proper job, getting a mortgage, buying a house, having children. Was he scared of being happy? No, he was scared of dying, and it made him squander everything. His money, his life, his time, even his health. Anya was the closest he'd come to a saviour, but surely there would come a time when she would realise the fundamental flaws in the man she had chosen. Short-term living wasn't her thing: she did everything she could to persuade him to give up his hand-to-mouth existence, yet he clung onto it as if it was existential freedom instead of a never-ending grind.

Anya took his arm as they left the restaurant. 'Are you OK? What are you thinking about?'

But Paul didn't reply. He didn't reply because he didn't want her to know that he was thinking about how long they could carry on like this. The answer was simple. Until everything they owned had been turned into money, and all the money was gone.

Katoushka

Salena Godden

Katoushka was on the train to Prague whilst the poet was already halfway towards Salzburg airport. The landscape heaved with life, with butterflies and deer, acres of wheat, corn and sunflowers. There was a river there, you could hear it. From Prague she would take the night train to Krakow and there she would visit the woman with the freckles in the old tea house.

Katoushka thought of home. She knew she was thinking of home because whenever she thought of home she could taste chicken, roast chicken. She was hungry. It was alright she was hungry as she had hastily bought a cheese and salad baguette at a kiosk in Linz train station.

At Salzburg airport departure lounge there was a Tibetan Buddhist monk in maroon robes. He was sitting alone reading a book, it was a paperback. Passengers hurried with boarding passes to queue at the gate. The poet sat and smoked and watched them stand in line. The poet thought it seemed pointless to stand and queue.

She watched them stand in line, hands on hips, agitating from foot to foot, passport in hand and ready, too soon, too ready. Eventually the gates opened and slowly passengers filed towards the plane runway, across the concrete. The poet and the monk were the last to board the plane, as they walked to the gate the poet thought the monk said something and she turned to see his face, it was a beautiful brown freckled face. It was the kindest face the poet had ever seen. The monk's eyes said something like a smile. The monk thought the poet smiled at him, so she did.

Katoushka thought about Austria. In Austria she had met the poet with hair like a lion and they had sat and watched the sunrise. The sky had been blushing above them whilst they swapped stories and burnt logs on the bonfire. They smoked roll-ups as the wood smoke curled into the mornings clear rose sky and they swigged red wine from the bottle knowing that they would meet again in London.

When the poet landed at Heathrow she thought about Katoushka on the train to Prague. The poet imagined Katoushka was probably playing her guitar and singing something in Czech or Russian or Polish. Admiring fellow travellers would tip and tilt their heads to listen to her lilting voice. The poet liked Katoushka's voice, it had made her tip and tilt her head too, tip and tilt her head, so the light would shine though Katoushka's chestnut coloured hair.

The poet was hungry and she thought about eating chicken, chicken or eggs. Boiled eggs with salt or chicken with pepper but she never ate the two together because that was like eating from the beginning to the end and she never knew which came first - which did come first the chicken or the egg? She pondered this and grew slightly irritated, partly because she was waiting for her luggage to arrive, partly because a red-faced child was crying loudly and shrill, partly because she wanted to smoke and it was forbidden, partly because she was very hungry but mostly she was irritated because she was thinking about that ridiculous chicken and the egg question again.

When Katoushka unwrapped her sandwich, she found it was not cheese and salad at all but egg salad with yellowing mayonnaise and cucumber. The cucumber was warm, like courgette, it was soured and it looked glazed and cooked. The sandwich must have been there in the hot sun all day, baking under the glass.

Katoushka screwed up her nose whilst she wrapped the sandwich back in the plastic cellophane and put it in the flip top bin under the window. She looked out of the window as night drew in there was a linear slither of pale blue daylight along the horizon. It looked like a drawing made by a child with a pin scratched in black wax, black boxes shaped farm houses, black mountains and trees, edged and outlined with daylight blue.

The poet finally got her luggage and made her way out of the airport and to the train platform. She saw the monk go through the other passport control, the one that meant he was not from Europe, his passport looked leather bound as a bible. The poet wanted to see his face as if it were nourishing, his face was the kindest face she had ever seen. She yearned to see his eyes just one more time to see what they would say, then she thought he could hear her looking so she looked at her flip flops and toenails, they were both turquoise. When she looked up to her great dismay he was gone.

When the poet got to the platform she found that the trains were not running and she would have to take a special bus to another station, presumably a special station. It was cold in England, everybody was agitated and people pushed past her to get on the bus when it was already full. They loaded their luggage in the hold when there were no seats causing terrible confusion. The bus driver was very tense, he repeated who's suitcase is this? A woman had lost her husband's coat and a young girl was demanding to board the bus as her bag was in the hold. One man was demanding to be let off the bus as his bag was still on the pavement.

The poet stood back to wait for the next bus. She didn't see the point in the urgency, the too soon too ready. She prowled and smoked and started to shiver a little. She reached into her bag and found some trousers, she pulled her jeans on under her short summer dress. A man watched her and he thought he saw a glimpse of her pants. Her skirt got caught as she struggled into her jeans and the man thought he saw a glimpse of her pants, the poet saw him think this and he looked away quickly, ashamed.

Katoushka took out her guitar and played gently. She sang a song in Polish, the woman with freckles had taught it to her in Krakow and now she was going to see her, to learn another song. Every time she visited the woman with the freckles in the tea shop she taught her another song to take away with her.

The song was a story of unrequited love. The woman in the song said love me like a wife and the king said but I already have a wife. The woman said then love me like a friend and the king said I already have too many friends. She continued, then love me like a stranger and the king replied we have too many strangers in this country. Then she said finally love me like a chicken and the king said if I loved you like a chicken I would eat you whole and the woman replied finally if you ate me whole you would have no eggs. Katoushka sang the song and it was of unrequited love and she sang it well, it would make you tip and tilt your head if you had heard it.

The poet is at Liverpool Street station. There are two girls with long hair and short skirts. One sits on the floor her face covered in hair kicking the other hard in the shin whilst she is on the pay-phone. The one on the phone rips at her hair and kicks her hard, still on the telephone. The commotion continues, like seagulls tearing at the stuff left by boats and there is no intervening to do. They kick and spit at each other and the poet hears a slap, a thump that resonates.

The railway guard lets Katoushka have a cheap student ticket. She is not a student although she is always learning. Two young people, a first love couple, get in the same carriage as Katoushka, she continues playing until she has finished her song. When she stops she finds they are speaking in Serb, Katoushka can understand the dialect and they give her a beer and bid her to keep playing. The sky is soaked with bright stars that tilt and tip their heads as she sings, her voice lilts and carries off through the train and into the night. The young Serb couple hold hands and tip and tilt their heads as she sings a song in Czech. The Serb boy has a wooden flute and he plays a song, it is a song about a mouse that thinks it is a lion.

There was once a tiny brown mouse, the boys says, he was the smallest mouse you ever saw. He had small brown ears and a tiny twitchy nose. He didn't believe he was a mouse however, he was utterly convinced he was a lion. One day he got caught in a mouse trap but he did not die because he believed a mouse trap is too small to kill a lion. Then he got cornered by the fat farm cat but he was not afraid and did not get hurt because he believed he was a lion. Lastly however a girl mouse falls in love with him, for her he is so attractive and courageous. However of course, he believes he is a lion and he cannot find love with a mere little brown mouse and he rejects her. The broken-hearted girl mouse sees him for what he is a brave little mouse with a lions heart, but he is forever always seeking his true love lione's, which of course he will never find in the skirting boards and rafters of the old farm house.

The poet is in a taxi from Liverpool Street station. She is hungry and she is eating a warm croissant. There are crumbs when she gets out and the taxi driver swears at her. He is irritable partly because the taxi was spotless clean and partly because he hates crumbs. Mostly though he is angry because he doesn't want to be a taxi driver he would rather be on television making people laugh. His friends think he is a very funny man and when he is in the pub he makes the barmaid laugh, he would rather be on television telling jokes and wearing a bow-tie than sweeping poet's croissant crumbs out of the back of his nice clean black cab.

The crumbs liked it best when they were a whole croissant, they are scattered in parts and are left, discarded in the gutter.

The poet scurries quickly into her home terrified, convinced the taxi driver will kill her. She is afraid, she finds London a very cold and irritable place, she wants to be in her bed. When she climbs the ladder to her bedroom, she discovers a trail of mice droppings along the skirting and under her bed. The mice are very clever, they must be able to climb ladders the poet thinks.

Katoushka is talking to the Serbs about the woman with the songs in the teahouse and they nod and want to meet her too. They too would like to learn another new song. The wooden flute is beautifully carved and the noise it makes is like a beating heart with the cells dividing. The carvings in the flute are whole stories and each time you play a note these stories are scattered into the smoke and air and up into the stars.

Now all the poet can think about is climbing out of her clothes and pulling her wiry heavy hair free, out of her tight ponytail. She wants to bury herself beneath the covers to sleep and dream of acres of landscape heaving with life, with multicoloured butterflies and wild deer, acres of wheat, corn and sunflowers. A place where there is a river and you could hear it.

Katoushka is sleepy. The train rhythm is a lullaby, like a mother's voice rocking you to sleep, whispering the song of the man in the moon, goodnight mister moon, come again and see us soon. The young Serb couple have fallen asleep with a tip and a tilt of their heads listening to her lilting voice and their bodies lean against each other like the happiest drunks. The flute is still in the boy's hand, the stories the flute has to tell rest for now in the grains in the wood carvings. Many miles ago the man who carved that very flute blows out his candle, wax smoke wisps up the chimney and into the star soaked night.

Katoushka dreams but she forgets her dream, she thinks she has a dream about a poet in London with hair like a lion. She thinks she remembers a poem about a lion that thinks it is a mouse.

Haraka

Shiromi Pinto

'Where is it?' He heard his mother's voice through the clink of Meccano pieces. His father he only heard in hushed tones. Murmurs. 'Who did you give it to?'

Her challenge sent little tremors across linoleum. He set aside the Meccano, and turned to the Lego blocks, which were lying in a mess of multi-coloured rubble on the carpet. He grouped reds and whites together, stacking them carefully to form a hollowed, rising square. Block followed block, slipping seamlessly onto the pegs beneath it, adding another layer to the foundation of the tower. He worked exclusively in red; white would comc later.

'There were two. Where is the other one?'

He rubbed the edge of a block, marvelling at its smoothness, and listened. Yes, he remembered, there were two. He turned toward the wall-unit, away from his parents' voices, and saw it there on one of the shelves. Just one, gathering dust in the thatch of its roof. A miniature ox pulling a miniature cart; the ox teased out of a chunk of light brown wood, the cart woven from varied widths of bamboo. It had arrived with them only a week ago, brought back from a holiday in Sri Lanka, its identical twin wrapped tightly beside it.

Haraka. When he looked at the boy, the word often crawled up his father's throat like phlegm. 'Haraka!' the boy would repeat out of ear-shot, flailing his arms in the garden. It became a battle cry, a siren call, even a prayer. 'Oh yeah,' he would say to the old lady next door, pumping his muscles, 'I am the Haraka.' He saw his first haraka on the side of the road as they drove from Katunayake airport to Colombo. It moved slowly, driven forward by a blind man's stick. The boy tugged at his mother, pointing at it, a question in his eyes. 'Haraka,' she had said, watching it lumber alongside, and the boy sat back with a frown. Haraka. When they left, they brought one – no, two – back with them from Sri Lanka. Wouldn't leave without them. His namesake twice etched from wood.

That summer he had spent long afternoons in Thalawatugoda, watching the ox in the field next to his uncle's; its slow munching jaw captivated him. In the evenings he wandered through paddy fields, flopping along mud welts following herons, often ending up at a pansal. There he would tip-toe furtively along its edges, peering into the temple to see whether there were any monks around. Satisfied that he was alone, he would leap up to the root of a banyan tree and swing. His face brushed and often collided with other hanging roots, so he would veer and spin his vine, sometimes in an attempt to avoid, sometimes not. If he wasn't in the mood to swing, he would recline on other roots which, through constant use, had been twisted into smooth seats. When the monks finally chased him away, he slipped down to the edge of a pond. Behind him, the sun melted into the paddy fields while water buffalo swam idly below.

The tower grew steadily in proportion. He was working in white now, brows furrowed as he calculated dimensions and numbers of blocks required. It was an exact science; all whites and reds would have to be used. But his eyes kept rolling toward the wall-unit. There had been two, he was quite certain of that; and his mother seemed very upset at the loss of one of them. Even he thought the ornament looked wrong on its own, driving calmly toward the edge of the shelf, dragging dust and mites with it.

'Who did you give it to?' His mother was asking again, and again his father gave a low decibel grunt.

His father was often harder spoken than that, looking at him from time to time, barking, 'Fat Apple' and chuckling. 'Hey, hey, hey, are you coming my way?' he was tempted to respond, but he would lower his eyes and slide into his bedroom instead. There he would look at himself in the mirror. In his green football shirt with its stretchy plastic fabric, he did look vaguely like a Granny Smith apple. He would turn away to contemplate his walls: the small white dimple by his mirror, chipped from light blue by his mother's teeth; and the model helicopter, a gift from his father, still waiting to be built.

But it was not the model that drove him just then. It was his tower. Or at least it would have been had he not been distracted by the missing ox-cart. He approached its counterpart again, fingering its beady eyes. They glinted like the nails he had seen in his father's eyes only a few weeks before. As their steel heads hardened against him, he had dropped out of sight, flinching into a corner of an almarya. Sitting in the wardrobe, knees pulled against chest, his back trembling against a hard wood wall. Outside he heard the steady snap of leather. If he looked, he knew he would see his mother curled like a prawn on the bed, a belt ricocheting off her back. Inside, sweat had gathered in slicks behind his knees and coasted down the backs of his thighs, stinging as it ran over welts.

'Don't come to interfere,' his father had said to him. But when he found him in the cupboard later that afternoon, he stroked his head. 'What have I told you? Haven't I always said not to poke your nose in our business?'

His father led him from the cupboard and hugged him. When the boy looked at him, the nails fell from his eyes, like shadows, into the palm of his hand. And the boy took the nails, clasping their warmth in his fingers, later pounding them into the hull of a coconut.

'Where is it?' His mother's voice shook loose cupboard and nails, prompting him to peek through the slats of the kitchen door. His father sat glaring wordlessly while his mother pursed and unpursed her lips.

The boy shuddered. There were times when his mother's lips lost control, bursting against her teeth, later blooming from her face like orchids.

'Run. Go. Run.'

Once these words had fallen like blood from her lips and he had fled, running down the hill of the front lawn, words pushing his feet forward. What had he done? His ear still rang from the blow that he had caught in his mother's place. 'Don't touch her,' he had cried, and then he was running. Away from the wind and the hiss of maple leaves. And the windows. Slamming shut one by one as leather slid from belt loops. Panes double-glazed with silence, reflecting sun and clear blue sky.

And he was still running. Where did he run to? He couldn't remember. But there were flowers everywhere, pink and falling from cherry trees, and leaves shaking like hands from branches. And behind him, orchids bloomed, leaving a white sliver on blue walls.

'Who did you give it to?' His mother clasped her hips with her palms. His father kissed his teeth at her and laughed.

'Just shut up, will you? Don't you remember there was only one bloody haraka?' The boy crept away from the kitchen door back to his tower of Lego. He glanced again at the wall-unit where the ox-cart continued its progress toward the edge of the shelf. He nodded.

Yes, perhaps there had only been one.

The Funeral

(Dedicated to the memory of Victoria Bellevue)

Barbara Graham

A bird's eye view would have seen us sweeping towards the church doors like ants. Identical beads of black, streaming towards a mound in the earth, some of us allowing ourselves the odd nod or greeting at the risk of not getting a seat. A funeral is the one occasion when the drums of the Caribbean beat to the tick of Greenwich Mean Time, and there's no avoiding being anything but embarrassingly late. Obeying the clock and once inside the undisputed hierarchy of pews, being not close but friends, we sat near the front of the rear section. Loosening shawls and removing scarves, we fixed our funeral clothes, and began simply remembering MaVic from the colour photo on the order of service cover. She looked happy. Smiling red lips, matching hat and patterned neck scarf, the image far from the old lady I'd seen at a wedding last summer. Yet it was a picture of the Antie with the mischievous tell tale eyes that I remembered.

We sat, waiting. The stillness of death stealing us away from the palpitating pace that would have continued yesterday. The church gathered us up into its open arms, reflected its stained glass and bestowed upon us the reminder that at the end of the day we are all sinners. All at once the seats filled; amongst the indistinguishable backs of heads and coats in every shade of black, three fair-haired white people stood out like albinos. This was a meant to be a celebration, yet we adorned the colour of mourning; custom punctuated by blond haired black girls, blue braids and a woman old enough to know better wearing a caramel coloured coat. I occupied myself identifying profiles and bald or bare heads and of course, there sat a few rows behind the resonant emptiness of the family seats, was Mistress Campbell (as everyone of her generation called

her. . . Some legacy of a reputation from back home that she'd never outlive), whose no doubt newly bought attire from her grandiose hat to matching heels, were more suited to a wedding than a funeral. I'd not seen her for years but still remembered her from Antie Doris's parties and wondered now if her increased age meant her stiletto heels had reduced in height, and if she still wore those colourful lurex low back dresses that Mum said in old age would give her a hunch back like the white people 'cos she neva have arn ves'.

A sudden hush and glance behind stopped my thoughts and judgments. The coffin passed by balanced by four of the six insistent male relatives of unequal height. The family followed two by two, silent, serious, seemingly serene. None crying tears, so why all of a sudden was I? Fears for the limited future decades of my 86-year-old mother, now sat beside me, meant I couldn't help but imagine how it must feel to be burying your mother. Or do you feel? Do you not become frozen in a state of doing like I did with Dad? Then some kind of primal emotion exploded through centuries and gripped the heart of me, nailed me to the seat in disbelief in the registrar's office, and rocked me back and forth as the shadows crept out of the a.m. hours and grief screamed out from deep within my gut. I heard my own self moaning a low, deep-rooted hurt that needed my Daddy.

A sermon, a solo, another hymn, tributes by sons. A baby on a grandmother's lap cries through eulogy. I'm struggling to listen and fill the years before we knew her. She came to England to be a nurse. I'm soon thinking about life and the growing up years when Mum and Antie were best friends, and all of a sudden I get it. I remember a time when she was laughing. I'm crying, Gwenny's dead! Mummy told me not to give her injection with the matches stick. Antie's laughing, so is Mum. They often laugh and sometimes I don't get it. Gwenny's dead! I used the burnt end and she said it hurt! The tale lived on to be told at the wedding, nostalgically around a table; how Gwenny drop sleep when we was playing doctors and nurses. I loved it when Antie told the back home stories. It was different from when relatives came and the grown ups got together and reminisced. I'd heard those stories so many times from my hiding place under the table, yet each time was like the first, told in broad accents between repeated choruses of laughter. I could still see Miss Vi getting married in the old time eyeglasses that her Granny leave her, because her Granny and Papa dem did married 52 years, before Papa dead pan top a de widow next door.

The baby's father puts all his embarrassment into styling his walk from the front pews, to rescue the baby from his mother's lap. The baby girl stops crying, but he continues past me to the back of the church. Grandma fixes her sixties wig, pulling it forward on her forehead with both hands. She wraps her button-less faux fur coat around her, secures the strap of her Dalston market Burberry hand bag and follows, hurrying apologetically.

Antie's stories were new and alive and exciting. I'd never heard them before. Stories of her childhood, like when the shortcut home from school cut the journey by half... but Mamma seh not to go dat way 'cause dem seh Mad Rolan tek up residence in a de gully an mek up camp. Well one day at school, Tut bet Man Man two june plum and one mango, seh im wouldn't tek de shortcut. Now, Antie and one nada girl name Glori, used to live in a de same district, was to wait pan de other side a de gulley to mek sure seh Man Man come tru an' neva cheat. Everyting arrange, Antie and Glori leave school an' head straight for home side of Mad Rolan gulley. Tut tek Man Man chalkboard, (cos if dat larse is more dan trouble) an' mek sure seh Man Man go tru school side. Den 'im was to wait until teacher leave school, to mek sure seh Man Man nuh double back, den run round goh meet dem an' walk home as usual.

'Bwoy what you doing dere? Is not time you reach home?' Teacher Williams rebuked

Styles Washington for hanging around after school, and gave him his cue to run round pass Orange grove and Mass Ferdi's headstone shack, over the stream, skipping every other. One of the discarded headstones with wrongly spelt names, (that is the ones such as Janie Simit, which Ferdi couldn't persuade the fambilies was passable for Smith,) tru midnight alley, pass crossroads and Miss Lou kitchen to meet Antie and Glori at the other side of Mad Rolan gulley, in the opening by the peeny wali bush. When 'im reach, him shirt wet wid sweat and 'im 'ave two board an' no chalk (dem would have to use rock stone tomorrow).

'What? 'Im nuh … come tru yet?' Tut blew, bent over and breathing hard.

'No, an' I'm not sure dis was such a good idea, Tut Washington.'

'No, yuh too deblish. Yuh shoulda neva mek him do such a ting,' said Glori.

'Man Man too craven fe food. You tell me Vicky. You woulda pass tru Mad Rolan gulley fi one even two mango and two june plum? Eh? ' Im too lub food'.

Glori was by the mouth of the gulley calling out to Man Man.

'Man Man Moses, where are you?'

Vicky and Tut joined her.

'Man Man!'

'Man Man!!'

'Man Man, where are you?'

'Oh Gaad, weh 'im deh?' said Tut, and Glori started to cry. One bwoy from school name Dalton Samuels (who used to be in dem class but dem keep 'im back in third grade tru 'im cyan spell) passed them on his way to Miss Lou kitchen.

'Unu nuh reach from school yet? Ah sure ah see yuh mada lickle way back a look fi yuh Glori.'

Glori started to cry again, 'cause she know seh she ah goh get beat'n' when she reach home. But dem couldn't just leave Man Man, even though none a dem neva goh dat way before it name shortcut, an' Tut wait after school an' goh de long way roun' and still Man Man cyan reach. Antie told us how one bwoy name Josiah Brown used to go that way an' reach home quick quick every day but him an' Rolan was cousin.

Anyway, Glori mada caught up with her by the mouth of Mad Rolan gulley and drapes her up, but she never talk. Learning it was more than past time, Antie an Tut followed not too far behind, trying to tink 'bout how they was going to explain to where they was, and where was Man Man Moses, and how they was going to get the story straight and communicate it to Glori. Tut told Antie how for the first time 'im mek mistake an step pan Calvin Grant headstone when he was running through the stream, an' 'im did know dat was a bad sign, and Antie told him how the last time her brother stepped on it, their Granny died sudden, an' 'im vow never to step pan it again, cause she neva sick. The story goes that Calvin Grant turned up at school the day before his funeral and no body would sit beside him, until 'im explain how 'im hear seh im dead, but im did gaan a St Elizabeth go 'look fi im other farder, but the next day im neva come back to school and only rumour seh im move gaan a foreign lef' 'im duppy.

All of a sudden they heard Dalton shouting 'Eh, whole arn dere! ... Eh Tut! Yuh fren Man Man deh back dere in a one state. Mad Rolan 'ave 'im outside a Miss Lou kitchen!' Antie looked at Tut and Tut looked at Antie.

'You gwan home, me a bwoy chile.'

Styles 'Tut' Washington ran like his mother was chasin' him, closely followed by Dalton Samuels, back to Miss Lou's Kitchen. There a bawling Man Man dangled by the collar of his now wet, button-less one school shirt, from the hook of Mad Rolan's middle finger. He saw Tut and started wriggling 'Aaah, loose me, loose me.' Rolan raised his hand higher and dropped the boy in a bony mound of green and gold mud camouflaged uniform. Then he let out one mad man laugh and run off in the direction of crossroads.

No one could tell what really happened in the Mad Rolan's gulley that day. Man Man claim seh Rolan promise 'im licks if 'im tell, and Tut claim seh is cause Mad Rolan' deh wid Man Man sister Rose why Man Man come out alive, an' 'im know de res' but cyan talk, but Man Man did pee-pee up 'imself. Antie said dat was de las' day Man Man Moses eva walk home wid dem, im start tek de shortcut tru Mad Rolan gulley and reach home fus. I wished, now I was old enough to be curious and ask questions, I could ask Antie what happened to Styles 'Tut' Washington, Man Man Moses and Glori. Did any of them come to England? And did Tut eva pay Man Man the two june plum and one mango?

Brother Morgan from the row behind passed me his kerchief, as the coffin was carried out. They say when an elder dies it's like a library burning down. Not wanting to witness the outing of these flames, I persuaded Mum not to go graveside. Outside, almost prematurely, the celebrations began. People gathering and taking time to say 'Howdy', discovering maiden and surnames to realise they were half-cousins and god brothers or god sisters on their father's side. My eavesdropping on the many conversations, while Tony went to get the car, interrupted by an old boyfriend going out of his way to say hello to me and Mum, as Mrs. Campbell clicked by in three-inch heels; my surprise at Gwenny not recognising me; and the lady in the caramel coat making the mistake of thinking I was family. Told me I have a resemblance and she just come from Jamaica yesterday, and how it cole an' she had was to borrow her sister-in-law coat, so we must forgive her, and by the way her name was Rose and tank you for coming. Once settled in the comfort of Tony's car I turned to Mum.

Mum, tell me stories Mum, the back home stories all of them, as many as you can remember.

The Race

Abby Ajayi

I controlled my tears well; even then, I was adept at holding my will and hiding it all.

It began when I was not invited. Nothing important you realise, but back then, aged 10 years old, everything was important. Every slight, every rejection real or imagined cut me to the quick, sent me into a tailspin, a maelstrom of tears, introspection and pounding, headache inducing fear. What did I do wrong? Ten years old and I was unable to comprehend why.

Why would she not invite me? I had been good to Andrea, helped her with her Maths, which I was good at, gave her one of my prized new pencils that Daddy brought back in a pencil case set from America. I wanted her to be my best friend. Why wouldn't she invite me? Everybody got to be Andrea's best friend for a time, first it was Susanne and then Tilly and then Annie and then Susanne again. Perhaps it will be my turn soon.

After almost a year in the school, this knocked me for six – words like ostracize and isolation meant nothing then. We had only been in England for a year and this was a new beginning for all of us, a new school, new house, new everything. I had embraced it all, this world, this land of dreams that everybody back home talked about in hallowed terms. This promised place. Already I was leaving that world behind, the heat, the chaos, the loudness, the brightness, the smoke, the darkness. Now this was my home. I had embraced Neighbours, pop music, corner shops, cold and fish and chips with gusto, I wanted to belong.

And yet here I was, the only one in class 2b who hadn't been invited to Andrea's party. Everybody had their invitations – boys and girls – pretty pink pages with instructions on how to get to Andrea's house in sunny Palmers Green, green leafy Palmers Green, just over the way, but somehow feeling like a world away.

All these years later, Debbie's vague words of explanation ring in my head. I hear my words to her.

'Why? Why won't she let me come?'

'It's the race,' Debbie says. 'The race.'

But sports day was months ago I thought. By now anger had given way to disappointment. I could not bring myself to ask more and so the moment passed. Why would Andrea be angry with me about sports day? In that single-minded way of mine, I turned it over, opened it, prodded and pried, investigated and still I could not understand. Why would the race make her angry with me? I came second. Carly, bad, angry Carly won and even she was invited to the party.

My mother's vague words linger too. My mother, always quick to tell me to wipe my tears and behave, yet this time she surprised me; she listened. You are different she said – this, cold implacable woman, quick to anger, seemingly impossible to please. And yet I remember for the first time, that day, a hint of gruff tenderness that I had never before seen, perhaps never seen since that day. She understands more than I, yet still I could not grasp what she meant, why was I different? What did she mean? Yet she too was vague, a state which was rare with her given as she was to unequivocal displays of anger.

And so the party came and went. That Saturday, a cardinal rule was broken in my house. Mum, who refused to buy fast food, brought me McDonalds and we never spoke again of Andrea. In the days following, at school, some mention would be made of the party and I would see Miss Deacon shush the others as though in quieting them she thought that anything could be changed.

Never again would I approach sports day with the enthusiasm that I had before – the race I would think – what could I have done wrong? Somehow I knew then that everything had changed. I was set apart, given nothing but pitying looks – no one wanted to be sullied by my difference it seemed. Then I was blind to what is so clear now. Ten years old and I had gone so long without seeing. In Lagos I did not understand this word race.

Soon I would understand all too well.

The Smell of Petrol

Nii Ayikwei Parkes

He woke up feeling complete; like a countable citizen of his country, a fully formed moth. He rushed through his breakfast with a smile on his face then streaked outside with a set of keys jingling on the third finger of his left hand. The key ring felt like his wedding band – something tying him to the realm of class. Till death us do part. It was July 7.

Owusu led a simple life. Loved his early morning breakfasts of boiled green plantain and speckled, spicy Egusi stew.

'A man who works with his hands cannot eat bread for breakfast,' he'd say as his wife, Amina, teased him about his appetite.

'And what about your daughter?' she'd retort, pointing at the younger of their two children, Efua, who at five had begun to demand the same palm-oil-rich breakfast as her father.

'Maybe she'll be a plant technician too,' he'd laugh. 'At least your son still breaks bread with you.'

'Hmm.'

Their banter ended with silent smiles.

At work, where he ran a soap cutting line, Owusu would break for lunch at 12.30 for another heavy meal. It was usually black-eyed beans stew with rice. In fact, his diet was identical to that of his brothers who lived up country. They were farmers, and he was always keen to stress how different they were. After all he worked in an industrial plant, while they tended the fields with their bare hands. He was a technician, the educated one. It was not that simple, but it is easy for leaves to forget the soil and praise branches for carrying them.

Owusu's children had never been to the village where he came from. Yaw, his son, had met his uncles and grandparents when they came to the city for Efua's outdooring, but since then there had been no visits. Owusu had been summoned and invited by his family but he had ignored the summons and forbade Amina to raise the subject. He said was working overtime and could not afford to leave the city when there was so much work. The other subject that Amina rarely raised was positioned on the left side of their two-bedroom house. It was covered with a large patchwork cloth made from remnants of fabric from their local tailor; tie and dye, Dutch print, and wax print swathes of varying colours, textures, shapes and sizes, rendered uniform by the anointing of dust.

Dust was a great equaliser in the city. All things were swiftly coated with a fine layer of dust. Aging them. De-glossing them. Making the flashy look ordinary, the new old.

Even the eager spirit and hope of new arrivals to the city was soon dulled by the power of dust. Owusu made the large patchwork cloth painstakingly. With his own hands. So that he could protect his most prized possession – a gleaming rust-patched cream Toyota Starlet – from the dust.

The inside of the car was impeccably clean, and he had installed an air freshener on the dashboard to keep the car smelling 'superb'. Beneath the bonnet everything gleamed with such brilliance that it was easy for the casual eye to miss the non-existence of a distributor, battery, and radiator cap. The car had never moved since he bought it. Indeed, to call what he bought a car was flattery of sorts. It was a shell with no tyres and half an engine. But Owusu jumped at the chance to buy his own car.

In the two years since, he had bought rims and tyres and lowered the brick-propped chassis onto the ground. He had replaced the hollowed out lights with working duplicates and re-attached the steering wheel. And, religiously, every morning he had cleaned the car until the rust looked out of place. To the outside observer it looked in perfect working order. Sometimes when they had guests, he would uncover the car for effect, but graciously desist from mentioning it until, occasionally, a guest would say:

'That's a well kept car.'

And he would respond, 'Yes, I'm very proud of it.'

Or his favourite guest comment;

'You are doing well ooh!'

To which he would laugh, scratch the left side of his head, and say, 'I'm trying, my brother, I'm trying.'

It was a source of constant amusement for Amina who, of course, knew the car had no legs. In the last year though, Owusu worked extremely hard; taking all the overtime he could get during holiday periods, and working late whenever his shift manager demanded. The extra money he earned didn't stray into Amina's pot or Yaw and Efua's wardrobe. He bought a brand new battery, Elephant brand because he had been told they were the best; a radiator cap; and, by luck, his friend Gyamera the mechanic found him a distributor from the wrecks of a recent accident. Gyamera was the only person apart from Amina and the children who knew about the car's disabilities; since he helped Owusu complete many repair missions. For his help in finding the distributor, and his silence, Owusu bought him a bottle of Henkens Aromatic Schnapps; a favourite of the harvest gods according to the elders.

On July 6, 2001, Owusu brought two gallons of petrol home and his leopard-cream Toyota Starlet tasted the fiery pink liquid for the first time in three years. In gratitude it responded to the ignition on the seventh try after much accelerator-pumping to feed its fuel lines. Yaw and Efua clapped when they heard the choke and splutter of the car. Amina smiled. Owusu revved enthusiastically then got down to retrieve something from the kitchen. He returned with a small can of black paint and proceeded to daub his name and address in tiny text on the right front side panel just behind the tyre, mirroring the fashion of the taxis that criss-crossed the city. Writing his name above the symbolic line that divided the well off from the hustlers. At night he dreamt dreams he had never dreamt before and woke up repeatedly to express his joy on Amina.

As he took to the road in the morning, there was something buried beneath his elation. Simmering as he put his key in the ignition with a silent prayer. Somehow in this moment he felt more passion, more fear than he had felt at his own wedding. More excitement than the first moment his hands had dipped below a girl's waist beads. The car responded with a mild shudder of acquiescence, then coughed and spluttered its way past the nameless green hedges that enclosed his compound. By the time it slid through the makeshift gateposts, it was humming like a dragonfly. Owusu waved enthusiastically to the silhouette of Amina as he cruised away from home.

It was only when he got to the city centre that he realised it was harvest time. Small groups of drummers and dancers lined the roads chanting rude songs about the fertility of the earth. Taxi drivers were honking their horns in unison, and hawkers were throwing in responses to the chants. The ensemble created a unique soundtrack for the city that had a trancelike effect on listeners. Owusu found it unbearably colourful and festive. He had not poured libation for the gods this year. He had even forgotten to give Amina extra money to prepare special food for the children, and any guests that might turn up. No wonder she had been so quiet during the week. He had forgotten the harvest!

Soon after exiting Equality Circle onto Link Road, he saw his old friend JoJo on the opposite side of the road and waved. It might have been the stench of Nnokware lagoon that distracted him, but it's hard to say. Nevertheless, between waving and turning onto Link Road, the proud cream Starlet crashed into the barrier alongside Link Road and ended up poised like a see-saw at the edge of the sewer that led into Nnokware lagoon.

Owusu got out of the car and held on to the door on the driver's side to try to keep it from falling into the sewer. It wasn't a steep drop and the car would survive, but Owusu held onto that door as if it was his breath. A small number of passers-by came to help him, but the car was gradually slipping away. By now a mob had gathered; a motley crush of men, women and children who had not anticipated this extra entertainment but were happy to watch. His helpers surmised that there was no saving the car and retreated to join the crowd in yelling at him to let go. It was only a matter of time before the car would drag its owner to a smelly end. Still he held on. Paralysed by something unnamable. The veins in his neck emerged like tree roots feeding the trunk of his neck. He looked up to the sky and heaved, and muttered, and swore.

Then he asked, 'Does anyone smell petrol?'

Tempting Faith

Dzifa Benson

It's true

The path of destiny is as large

As my ever erect penis

I am first among gods

Conductor of Enlightenment

And always ready to fuck

I personify the hope and perils

That open the way of brand new channels

Skirting the abyss of chaos

I use my phallus to make a bridge

So that mortals don't fall in the drift

Mine the symbols of child, dog and walking stick

Mine the realm of opportunity

Mine the essence of potentiality

The eternal wanderer

I quiver on the threshold between light and dark – call me chiaroscuro

I prance between exterior and interior – call me omnipresent

I dally on the fine line between past and the future – call me timeless

I flirt with the edges of beginnings and endings – call me Janus

I interface impulses male and female – call me androgynous

I dance with the space around conflict and resolution – call me oracle

Tame and wild

Silence and speech

Human and divine

Young and old

Hot and cold

Peace and war

Rich and poor

I know them all

Primal as hunger

Fluid as quicksilver

Metaphysical as the ether

Elemental as promethean fire

I was, I am, I will forever be

The one who tricked you - Aflakete.

Many, many years from now, the door of a café in Holland Park clangs open and everybody's head, without exception, swivels round. A black man, age indeterminate, legs akimbo and leaning on a walking stick is framed in the doorway and sizing up the café. He enters with a smooth, undulating gait that belies any kind of disability implied by his use of a stick. The edges of his person are amorphous, indistinct, like an old black and white photograph fading to sepia. It appears the only way he remains upright is by the sheer cohesion of his body cell mass.

Senanu Gikunoo is the only occupant at a table that seats four in the otherwise packed café so the man makes a beeline in his direction. Senanu is dismayed. He is pretty dejected as it is and would prefer to stew alone in his own juices. As the man pours himself into the scat opposite and settles in, Senanu's nostrils are assaulted by a papery, desiccated smell that makes him think of old people. He chances a glance. Twinkling eyes playing hide and seek with a smirk stare straight back at Senanu and seem to bore through his eyeballs to examine the thoughts at the back of his skull. Senanu shifts his body so that he is oblique to the man and going back to his notebook, attempts to harness language in an emotional charge that will chime through the years in clear, precise poetry.

He writes:

The future has dimmed from bright to night

It's as sad as twilight and as decisive as midnight

Behind me are the shadows and embers of a stone cold hearth

Before me beacons to light the way of possible paths

But for now all I see is trouble and strife

As I contemplate this crossroads of my life

'By all the gods hold dear, would you please spare me the self-indulgent claptrap?'

It takes a couple of beats for Senanu to register that he is being spoken to.

'What?'

'I said –so change the''

'I heard what you said but what do you mean?'

By now the man's smile resembles that of a wolf eyeing up a lamb chop. He raises his chin, indicating the notebook. The width of the table between them, Senanu's side turned body and the notebook balanced on his upraised knee all inform Senanu that the man cannot possibly read his notebook from where he is sitting.

'Wanna bet I can't read it? Rhyme all you like, procrastinate, ponder, you've still got a decision to make.'

Senanu is taken aback. 'Who are you and what do you know about my decision?'

'You must know who I am. You invoked me. I am the Guardian of the crossroads, Keeper of the gates, Linguist of the gods, Opener of the way – '

Senanu interrupts him with a snort. 'I invoked you? What are you? The second coming?' Silently he adds, we've got a live one here.

'Mock if you will but I am very much alive. Your name is Senanu isn't it? Did you know your name means god gives things?'

Alarm, greasy and effervescent, shimmies up Senanu's spine, over the back of his head and hovers just above his crown ready to clamp down in clean cut fear should things turn tricky.

'Easy, easy now. Okay. Here's a clue. Last night you were reading about a blues man from a couple of centuries back, Robert Johnson, who met the devil one night at a crossroads in the bayous of Louisiana. Well, I am the one who met young Bobby. Sure, I can be a little devilish, okay very devilish sometimes but I am not the devil. Old Beelzebub had too much of a one track mind and lacked the finesse to strike a deal as sweet as the one I struck that night.'

Senanu can barely believe the words he is about to utter. 'Eleggua....you are Eleggua?'

This time the man's smile is beatific and his appearance seems to gels more into focus.

'What was it old Willie Rattle-a-Javelin said – a rose by any other name would smell just as sweet – though I prefer to be called Legba. You can even use my nickname, Aflakete if you like. I've been called all sorts. St Peter because of the keeper of the gates thing, obviously, which I don't mind. He gave me shelter from prying eyes a couple of times but I've always been a lot more fun to hang out with than that bible thumping bore. Some call me Loki. I like his style, but who wants to freeze their ass off in Scandinavia? Others call me Anansi – web spinning is definitely my forte. Some have called me Hermes. Eloquent, reckless Hermes. He was my brother in arms you know, but I ask you this – when was the last time you saw a man running around with winged sandals? I warned him that his bloody footwear would be the cause of his demise. My look is innocuous enough as you can see but a lack of mortal belief is beginning to do me in too. I've wasted time and now time is wasting me. I used to lay ladies who lunch in London, noodle nubile nymphs in Nubia, pacify pent up princesses in Persia…'

Senanu's eyes drop down to the spot where, if the table hadn't been in place he'd have been eyeing up Legba's crotch. Legba lets out a laugh so full of life it rolls over Senanu like thunder. Senanu looks around the café. A few people look over quizzically. But for the most part languid adolescents still loll in standard issue plastic furniture and nannies coo at their charges, twittering at each other. When he looks back towards Legba, the sight that greets him threatens to shake his soul loose from its casing. It's

Wile E. Coyote. Complete with toothy, cheese eating grin. Senanu knows who it is because he is presently doing a PhD in Classic Cartoons of the 20th Century and the Wile E. Coyote ones are his favourites. He scans the café again. To his immediate right is a clump of oldies - the blue rinse panthers as Senanu dubs them – who have congregated to eat cake, sip hot, sweet tea and debrief on the day's skirmishes. But they haven't noticed this new turn of events. After another thunderclap of a laugh Wile E. Coyote morphs back into Legba.

'I see you've heard about my infamous phallus? The path of destiny is indeed large like a penis. People in Dahomey used to sculpt me with that huge erection but I'm pretty normal sized. For a god. Used to get me mixed up with Pan a lot though – you should have seen the tackle all thosc pagans put on that randy old goat. But his libido was too voracious, he spoilt it for me so something had to be done about him. I despatched his pipe-troubling ass back to Olympus. Now he's deadpan, heheheheheh… I know his parents Hermes and Aprhodite will surely forgive me… Heheheheh…"

His laughter trails off.

Senanu isn't looking so tickled. He's looking even less unnerved. 'You're running scared,' Senanu says. 'Afraid you going to fade away like the rest of them? You carp on about mortals losing faith but you guys move the goalposts all the goddamn time. Seeing is believing and without us you are nothing.'

All traces of mirth have vanished from Legba's face. Something flickers across his expression, perhaps a fleeting acknowledgement of the veracity of Senanu's judgement. Then he becomes inscrutable, just as a proper god should look.

'Anyway we've got new, more reliable gods now,' Senanu continues.

'And just who would they be?'

'Well...we've got Lucre, Mammon, Cyberon. Even old Bacchus is still knocking around because he likes to party. And so do we.'

It's Legba's turn to look dejected and his visage shifts a little more out of focus. 'I see. In other words, blind faith in fakes.'

'They get the job done, know their place and don't fight amongst themselves. That's good enough for me.'

'Yup. Good enough if you're happy to settle for insincerity, aridity of imagination and consumerism run amok.'

'Why are you here?'

'I am here to restore your faith. You need to get closer to your true self. I am here because I want to be more than just an idea, get closer to my true self. Even gods need to love and belong.'

'You're here to restore my faith? Ha! You and whose pantheon?'

Legba gives Senanu a long, considered look then he says, 'We've digressed for long enough. All I can say is that when faith becomes blind it dulls the soul, withers and dies. In another few days your friend with the kidney problem isn't going to be well enough to cope with a kidney transplant and then he will definitely die. What have you decided? Does he get one of yours?'

'You know that my health is in the balance. I may not be strong enough to go under the knife for Miles. Besides, Grace, my wife, swears that if I do go ahead with the operation she will leave me, taking my kids with her. I don't want Miles to die but I don't want to lose my life or wife either.'

'You have to choose.'

'How can I?'

Legba is implacablc. 'You must.'

Senanu is put in mind of the quotation: when the gods wish to punish us, they answer our prayers. He searches Legba's face for its oracular nature but it remains as impassive as a sphinx's. He looks around the café but the teenagers' faces throw up questions for which they cannot yet know that there will never be answers. The militant elders are revealed to be nothing more than what they are – frail, mortal and rheumy eyed from peering closely at questions and never finding answers.

'I can't live to see Miles die,' says Senanu finally.

Legba's smile is now as indulgent as a parent's. He is so much in focus Senanu can see the individual pores on his face. 'You choose well. Grace isn't as graceful as you think.'

Senanu's head bows with the weight of his choice.

'Now,' says Legba briskly. 'I'm going to fix it so you don't have to choose. So that your friend will get better, you'll get better and you get to keep your family."

Senanu's head snaps back up. 'What!'

'It will cost you. You're vegetarian I know, but the cost will involve animal sacrifice.'

'Tell me, tell me, what do I have to do?'

'We'll get to that later. But I need your word that you will fulfil your side of our little bargain.'

'You've got my word.'

'Because if you renege on this deal, the consequences will be terrible for you and yours. Remember Robert Johnson dying very young from poisoning? Your fate will be far worse than that, believe me.'

'I believe you and I believe in you.'

'Okay then. Meet me here, same time, in exactly a month from now and I will tell you what's next. When you leave here today, go to the hospital, go and see your friend. I promise you everything is alright.'

And with that, Legba sashays out of the café. An instant later something occurs to

Senanu and he rushes to the door to try and catch him. But all he finds are the English clichés of a peaches and cream child gambolling with a black labrador dog on the verdant lawns of the park.

The Afghan Rug

Steve Porter

She arrives at the Kensington apartment early one summer's afternoon, in 1925, following closely on a most urgent telephone call. A stout, but commanding figure in grey and magenta, topped by a pill-box hat with an arrangement of imitation glazed cherries falling over the rim into her field of vision.

With a poised complacency she lowers herself onto the small sofa, removes her hat and cloak, the fullness of which she uses to cover over the floral cretonne pattern of the upholstery. As the widow of a former agent of the foreign office, Aunt Millicent has no inclination to modern tastes.

We are obliged to sit and wait for our esteemed visitor to announce the reason for her visit, as she takes off her coat and places this on the sofa next to her, arranging the folds into a fan like pattern to show the superior quality of the material.

'Harrods!' she snaps, upon finishing this, the remark exploding from like the sound of a muffled gun-shot.

Father, engaging with the unexpected drama that is now unfolding before him, raises a concerned eyebrow.

'Harrods?'

'Yes, Lewis, Harrods. My Afghan rug. You know the one. I'd like you to come with me to insist that they look into the matter at once.'

Aunt Millicent then proceeds to tell a very sorry tale that involves a complete lack of respect for her position as a lady, on the part of the staff, and a decline of standards that if not checked will almost certainly spread and have dire repercussions for the whole empire.

A cab is called immediately and pretty soon, Aunt Millicent is delivered to the offending establishment. Father hands her down from the carriage and leading her to the entrance with me following closely behind, my presence having been insisted upon by my Aunt as an essential part of my education, to show me the correct way of dealing with such situations.

Together we enter through the swing-doors, Aunt Millicent's umbrella swinging from her arm, the point of which is sharp enough to deal with anyone that would even think of getting in her way. Father too emboldens himself, ready for the task ahead of him as we make our way past the haberdashery section to the carpetry department.

Upon our arrival at the counter father taps on the desk with the habit and resolve of his former Rear Admiral command. In his past he has represented two brother officers in Courts Martial and with conspicuous success and so he knows of the considerable influence that his holding himself erect will have upon the slender, well groomed, but inexperienced young man standing before him.

The young man responds with a polite, but enquiring look in his eye.

'This lady,' announces my father, gesturing to his left, 'is my own dear sister, Mrs Millicent Collis-Watson.'

He pauses a moment, impressively, leaving the importance of such a statement for the young man to deduce for himself.

Aunt Millicent, in keeping with this, inclines her head slightly to the left causing the imitation glazed cherries to gather together into a discreet rustle.

A chair is bought over by a more junior employee and the young man behind the counter offers this to Aunt Millicent, who lowers herself into this slowly and with all the dignity that her situation merits.

'My sister,' continues father, when Aunt Millicent is comfortable, 'telephoned your department earlier this afternoon.'

'Forty-five minutes ago,' amends Aunt Millicent, sharply, bristling and ready for the fray.

It is a part of my education of which I thoroughly approve.

'Exactly,' acknowledges father, somewhat annoyed, it seems, by the unwarranted interruption, 'forty-five minutes ago, to enquire as to the situation concerning her beloved Afghan rug. You have had this for cleaning for nearly a month now and she quite rightly feels that it should have been returned.'

Aunt Millicent is now shifting from side to side in her chair, opening and shutting the clasp of her handbag and muttering to herself.

'However,' and this is said by father with the utmost gravitas, 'when my sister telephoned forty-five minutes ago, she was informed by someone in your department that the order could not be traced. I am therefore here with her to demand that you deal with this most unacceptable situation and with the utmost urgency!'

'Quite!'

The young man excuses himself then with due deference and plunges with commendable application into several order books, emerging shortly afterwards with a pale facc turning a delicate shade of pink.

'may I have Madam's full address?' He asked.

Father opens his mouth to speak but Aunt Millicent is there before him.

'158a Linden Avenue, West Eight.'

Father looks at Aunt Millicent with disdain, but she brushes the attempted reprimand away with a casual, almost inconsequential wave of her hand.

As the young man continues his search, turning deeper in colour as the seconds turn to minutes, the point of Aunt Millicent's umbrella can be heard tapping on the parquet floor with increasing regularity.

'Harrods!' she exclaims.

Father looks at the floor then, and then at me, as if to share his frustration, but I am so completely in awe of Aunt Millicent's command of the situation that I cannot even acknowledge him.

'I certainly didn't expect. I mean this is Harrods. Lewis, I think...'

But father cuts her short, his chest pushed out, and with his stature increased by at least two inches by the straightening of his back, he looks the unfortunate young man squarely in the eye.

'I think,' he says, 'that it is now time for us to see the manager of this department!'

The young man nods and after a subdued request to be excused, hurries off to find his superior.

'In an establishment of this standing!'

She addresses not only father and myself, but the whole of the department for added effects, her voice gaining volume and strength with every word and my father now obviously wholly perplexed as to how he can take charge of the situation.

By the time the manager arrives hurriedly, yet retaining his dignity, Aunt Millicent is fully launched on a damning critique of the service shown her, the way she has been treated and the decline of standards such as she has not seen since being stationed in Belgium.

'Twenty-five years I have been coming to this place. Never before have any of my orders gone astray. You just don't expect such a thing from the most highly regarded emporium of the empire. What has happened to my beautiful Afghan rug that I so trustingly left here in your keeping?'

The manager coughs in response.

'Madam,' he says. 'I myself have never known an order to go astray. Believe me when I say that I am deeply, deeply shocked and share your concerns. The matter, I assure you will be looked into thoroughly and immediately. I can only beg of you to excuse me that I may put a search of the entire shop into progress.'

Aunt Millicent sits back in her chair, championing her cause repeatedly with the full weight of her disgust 'disgraceful', she complains. 'it is simply beyond belief...Harrods, of all places.'

In due course, the manager returns and coughs again, reaching for the telephone. 'Madam, I will contact our delivery department. I now have no doubt that the order must have somehow by-passed our usually precise records and your rug will be ready.

But the delivery department has no record either, there appears to be no trace of Aunt Millicent's beautiful Afghan rug.

After much consternation and numerous apologies from almost everyone in the chain of command, it is finally agreed upon father's suggestion that the matter be left in the Manager's hands for the next two days, after which, if no further progress is made then the whole affair be referred to the proprietor for appropriate compensation.

This done with courtesy and despatch, father expresses his satisfaction, and much to the relief and surprise of the manager and young man that first served her, so does Aunt Millicent, following an uncharacteristic period of silence during the negotiations that father puts down to obvious strain that this has placed on her and the loss that she has suffered.

'Perhaps it has caused her a good deal more strain and worry than any of us realise,' he says, but I am not so sure, thinking now of all the power she exerted over father as much as the rest of them, a different path of distinction than that of my own earlier aspirations, but certainly one of her own choosing and to be admired for the strength of character it requires.

We are soon travelling again along the Brompton Road, past the Oratory and the museums, and then turning into Queens Gate, father, obviously saddened to see the small, frail and rather deflated Aunt Millicent. But as we pass the Albert Hall, Aunt Millicent meekly raises her head.

'I've been thinking Lewis,' she says. 'You know I wonder if, after all, it might have in fact been Harvey Nichols?'

Do Good by Stealth

Martin Ouvry

First rule: no trainers; a pair of proper shoes is what you want. Oh, trainers are great for walking around, and you might - at a pinch - get away with some seriously heavy, top-of-the-range, hundred-and-thirty-pound jobs. But nothing shabsville, nothing grot. Traditional shoes, solid, sober, clean, brown or black, leather or suede, your choice. Something not dissimilar to these, dare I say it. 'Cause when the time comes they'll look at that, narrow their eyes and judge you on it.

I was going to say jeans are equally a no-no. But then, jean technology's come a long way since whatsisface got naked in a laundromat to the strains of a Chicago preacher man. No, jeans should be fine, as long as they look respectable or scream boutique from every super-low-rise boot-cut stitch. Though proper trousers are a safer bet. Don't these make me look older, more responsible? The last thing you want is your scabby old sky-blues with bits hanging off them at the heel. That's why a shirt is a good thing: a shirt with a collar, to add a bit of dignity, show them you're a team player, a part of the mainstream. When it's time to make contact with a member of staff - I'll come back to this in a minute - a collar will remind them who's the boss.

The coat - ah, the coat - that's the crucial bit of kit. I use this big black thing in the winter months: it's naturally bulky, and the pockets are let into the lining, see? Invisible on the outside, and deep, very deep. Flaps, yeah? and horizontal zips, so they'll hold their shape, even when you're really loaded down. (If you're wearing gloves, tuck them somewhere else. Same goes for your keys. Don't clutter up your primary storage facility). They're quite low down, these pockets, on account of the coat's quite long, so you don't have to stick your elbows out when you're dropping the goodies in. Which is important: you can't go waving your arms around - they look at what you're doing with your arms. The sleeves are slightly overlong and loose-ish-fitting: it's an XL, an extra large; I got it in the sales. And it looks expensive, which it would have been. . .

The weather has to be right, of course: mild day's no good for a monster like this. Needs to be cold, though not necessarily raining. It's seasonal work, to a degree - although in England you never can tell what the weather's going to do from one day to the next, even at the height of summer, even if you trawl the forecasts. Remember Michael Fish, what he told us that November?

Make sure you've had a shave and washed your hair: there's no point wearing the uniform if you look like you're coming down from some mad all-nighter in Clapham North. Clean-shaven, that's the way to go - unless it makes you look especially young. Youth is not an advantage in this line of work: the youth are a high-risk category. Because of which, better not be chewing gum: in some people's eyes a little thing like that still smacks of teenage rebellion.

Ready to go, then, and in through the doors. Pick up a trolley - a trolley's far better than a basket - one of those shallow ones, if possible, so your shopping isn't engulfed. With a basket you have to keep swapping hands; and like I said, watch the body language, unnecessary gestures are out - you're not on stage at the National now, Clytemnestra. Then off you glide, cool, relaxed, unflustered, like a perfect little Stepford wife. After all, you will be on TV.

Which is why it pays to know the layout in advance. It's no good glancing around the whole time to see where the cameras are - they'll single you out in a shot. You've got to learn the angles, like a game of 3-D pool; suss out the blind spots, there won't be more than one or two.

Need to? Of course not. Almost nobody really needs to - they could give up the fags instead! No. Nine times out of ten it's a risk thing, adrenalin, the buzz as much as anything, that's the conclusion I've come to. The getting away with it, the act, that's what it's about. So case the place beforehand, the angles and the blind spots, and it may well spare your blushes.

Gauge the number of people in the store. Though this can work both ways: if the place is busy, you're less likely to get noticed; if it's empty, there's less danger from plain clothes. But there's still the cameras either way - and the eyes behind the lenses in that room behind the scenes.

Time of day. The human mind and body are at their least alert at dawn and dusk. But I'd say go at lunchtime or during the after-work rush, so you look like you've come from your upstanding job in the office.

Carry a shopping list in your hand. If there's a clip on your trolley don't use it. You'll need a list, not only for the obvious, but also to act as a decoy - to accustom the watchers to the fact that you've got something - innocent, legit - in your hand. That way, when you make the switch, they won't think anything of it. A shopping list is traditional, too; and more a female thing. Statistics say that a man is four times as likely to shop without one than a woman is. So a list says organised, disciplined. And make sure it's long enough so you can put a bit of clutter in your trolley. Biggish things: a loaf of bread, a pint of milk - bottle of wine's always good, or Cava's even better - to show them you've got money to splash on life's little consolations. Some salad stuff - avocadoes: luxury goods, again. Then you can get going. Pick what you really fancy: couple of pounds of peppered steak medallions at eleven quid a kilo; a pint of Madagascan tiger prawns. Get something cheap and cheerful, too: some bangers or streaky bacon. Don't put them in the trolley straightaway when the butcher and fishmonger hand you the bags; just glide off again, hugging the shelves so the cameras front and back of you lose sight of your right hand - or wait till you come to a blind spot, if no one's hanging around. Raise your shoulder, just an inch or two, and let one bag drop into your deep invisible pocket while cradling the other in your palm. Then put this one - the bacon or the bangers - in the trolley, in a highly visible position. No one will know the difference. And you can do it till you're bursting at the secret seams, as long as your trolley's filling also.

Now approach a member of staff - a stacker, a manager, whoever. Bring some variety to their day, give them something new to do, some healthy contact with their public. Act a bit helpless. Ask for directions to the carrots, say. They get to see your winning smile, smell your pricy aftershave, check out the shirt, the trousers, the shoes. Other staff will notice and remember their duty of service. Keep your friends real close is what I'm saying.

Proceed to the checkout. Make a show of your wallet or purse, your preferential plastic from a well-known high street bank, and the store card that tells them you belong. Make with the smiles; share a joke if possible. Ask for cash back, twenty pounds or so. And last but not least, take your time leaving. Sit down on one of the chairs beyond the checkouts, put away your cards and rearrange your shopping. Look leisurely. Act natural. Remember they can't get you anyway till you've actually left the premises. Then head for the exit, scouring the receipt for value and mistakes, and cast around now - absently, carefully - for signs of increased activity among the uniformed staff at the doors.

Then out you wander, nice and calm, like you're doing the most natural thing in the world. No sudden movements, don't quicken your step . . . just walk up behind them, touch them on the shoulder, and say 'Madam, would you step back inside the store with me please?' No fuss, no heavy stuff - not unless they make a run for it. They'll come quietly almost every time. And that's where you guys step in.

So, how am I doing? Can you give me a hint? I want this job, believe me. I reckon I'd be good, don't you? How do I look? Have I thought of everything? Put yourself in their shoes, that's my theory - just like when you're learning a part. I'm sure the acting training will come into its own. I mean, I know I'm kind of over-qualified, but I haven't had an acting job in, oh, six months, and I've definitely had it with that game. Had it with signing on, too. Have you ever been on the dole? You wouldn't believe how demeaning it is standing in that queue. Going through that shit every fortnight makes you feel like a bloody criminal. I've got a friend who's a sausage-buyer for Sainsbury's. She went to Oxford and she loves the job. A sausage-buyer. Oxford. What I'm saying is I'd get along fine. Put yourself in their shoes and you'll spot the buggers every time.

So, what do you think? Seriously. Can you let me know now? Am I in?

Note: The title of this story is stolen from Henry Fielding's Dedication of Tom Jones to his virtuous yet modest patron: 'Do good by stealth, and blush to find it fame.'

Island 21

Tom Lee

The island is not large, about a mile from end to end, the shape of a cashew nut. The shore is rocky except for the small pebbled beach on the inside curve of the nut, where they landed three months ago. The land rises and falls in a way that the conscript, in his letters to his sweetheart, has described as hills, although he knows it to be an exaggeration. The land is not – has never been – cultivated. The soil is dark and hard and for the most part there are only a few shrubs and bushes so non-descript that he would be surprised if they even had names. At one end however – the southern end? – there is a copse of trees. Here he has dug a toilet. The island is the kind of place, the conscript has often thought, where you might find the fossilised remains of a dinosaur.

The day of the invasion was triumphant. They had argued boisterously about the exact centre of the island and then planted the flag. He still remembers how vivid, how bold, its colours were against the grey sky, the brown earth. That evening they built a fire and roasted a pig that had been brought in anticipation of the mission's success. There was drinking and rowdy singing. The senior officers told stories of other battles, other campaigns, in which they had played roles. In the morning everyone had sore heads and wasted no time in packing up their equipment. He watched them, packed into the flotilla of brightly coloured fishing boats, until they disappeared from the horizon.

The conscript is serious about his duties. He sits now, at dawn, in his camp and takes apart his gun. He lays out the parts, the barrel, the trigger mechanism, the handle, the cartridge compartment and the sight. He pours fluid from a tiny bottle onto a soft cloth and, beginning with the barrel, carefully cleans each component. For the inside of the barrel, and other parts he cannot get to with his fingers and the cloth, he has pipe cleaners. He is thorough and takes his time. He handles it delicately, reverently, as if it were a woman, or a child. Then he reassembles it, oils the trigger mechanism and ensures that the sight is aligned to the barrel. The gun is a new model, imported from overseas.

It has only ever been his gun. It smells of its newness, and has never been fired.

In the past month the conscript has learnt the value of ritual and routine. Alone on the island, it would be easy to become lazy or careless in his habits, but it is in precisely situations such as this, his training has taught him, that he must remain efficient and alert.

After he has cleaned his gun he runs once around the island. Every 100 yards of the course he has marked a rock with a cross of boot polish. He has a rule that he must touch each of these rocks as he runs, so that he is not tempted to cut corners. It takes him nineteen and a half minutes to run around the island. Or it used to until a week ago when his watch stopped. Now he has a new system. This morning, before he sets off on his run, he builds a fire and puts a pan of water on to boil. When he gets back, breathless, he is pleased to see the water simmering, bubbles rising like drops of mercury from the bottom of the pan to the top. He knows that if he had not maintained a good speed the water would have been boiling by the time he returned. Equally, if there are no bubbles, the water is still calm, then he has run too quickly. It is the consistency that is important to him.

There is something reassuring about his ability to run around the island in this time. He feels that it gives him a certain authority over the territory to which he has been assigned. Now it does not take him nineteen and a half minutes to run around the island. It takes the time it takes to bring the water to a simmer. It is arbitrary, he knows, but it is something.

Once he has caught his breath he walks to the pebbled beach and takes off his uniform. He folds the clothes and puts them in a neat pile beyond the level of the high tide. He places his boots next to his clothes. As he walks down the beach he looks forward to the shock of the freezing water on his skin. He washes carefully. He gets the dirt out from under his finger and toenails. He is as thorough with himself as he is with his gun.

The maps and information he was given prior to the invasion refer to and describe Island 21. There was no information regarding islands one to twenty or twenty-two and above. He is curious, now, about the existence of these islands, though at the time he had not thought to ask.

The sun is high and hot. The conscript sits in his uniform and scrolls through the dial on his shortwave radio. He would like to hear news about the progress of the military campaign or the election that was imminent when he left the mainland. Occasionally he hears words in the language and accent that is familiar to him. He cranes his head towards the speaker, the muscles of his face tensed, but the voices are quickly blotted out by a rising distortion. He is able, of course, to pick up the incomprehensible voices and music of foreign radio stations. For these the reception is perfect.

He tries to write a letter to his sweetheart. When he first arrived on the island his letters were high-spirited, describing in meticulous and enthusiastic detail the geography of the island and his daily routine. Also, he would write down erotic fantasies that he had dreamed up involving his sweetheart, things that he would never have dared to suggest or describe to her in person. But today, when he tries to write his letter, all he has are questions, banal questions: How is the weather with you? Is there a new government? Is your mother's health still poor? And he squirms and gasps out loud when he remembers the appalling scenarios that had titillated him only
a few days ago.

He writes first of all, let me apologise for my long absence. He pauses. He writes the sun is high and hot. Just then the flag flying above the camp catches his eye - he is reminded that it needs patching. After a minute he puts the letter away in a wooden box. He takes out the small bottle of fluid, the soft cloth and the pipe cleaners, and begins to clean his gun.

The conscript is wearing only his starched white regulation underpants and waiting for the water to boil for his morning tea. His uniform is drying on the beach. After his morning run (when he had returned to the camp he had been disconcerted to find the water boiling furiously in the pan) he had bathed in the sea and then decided to wash his uniform. He had used stones to scrub it clean and then laid the pieces out flat on the beach. He had brought his boots to a deep shine and then placed them next to the uniform.

He is not boiling the same water that he heated during his run around the island. He knows that tea should not be made with water that has already been boiled. He cannot remember if he read this somewhere or if someone told him – his mother perhaps, or his sweetheart? – and nor, when he asks himself, does he remember the reason why. Whatever the source, the accuracy, of this piece of information, it has hardened into a truth, an article of faith. He makes his tea with fresh water.

When the water is boiled and he has made the tea, he adds a little sugar. The conscript is very particular about how much sugar he adds. If there is too little he cannot bear the bitterness. If there is a fraction too much it becomes too sickly for him to drink. He begins by adding far less than he knows he needs. Then he sips it and adds a little more. If it becomes too sweet he throws the tea away – the liquid loops through the air before disappearing into the earth – and makes another cup. Today he only has to make three cups before he has one that he can drink.

His bowels are loosened pleasantly by the tea and instead of going to the beach to put his uniform back on he walks to the copse of trees at one end of the island to relieve himself. He begins to read the thriller that he has already finished many times whilst sitting here. He enjoys it more each time he reads it. The plot fits together well, like a jigsaw, or a machine, and everything in it that happens, happens for a reason. There is action and intrigue and the characters are full of recognisable virtues. However, each time he has read it he has become more and more frustrated at the book's ending, which he considers a betrayal of the whole story. Last week he wrote a letter to the author expressing this opinion. He has even considered rewriting the final chapter himself - he has a very clear idea of how it should go.

Sometime later he arrives at the pebbled beach and finds that his uniform – his freshly cleaned clothes and shiny boots – are gone. A faint impression shows where the heavy waterlogged material had lain, the shape of a headless man.

It is several days – four? Five? – since his uniform disappeared. At the time he had considered, briefly, what might have happened – the wind perhaps, or a freak wave, even a mischievous seabird – but he has refused to let this setback interfere with his duties. Today, as every day since his arrival on the island, he marches up and down in front of his camp. He marches thirty paces and then turns and marches thirty paces in the opposite direction. He marches back and forth twenty times and then comes to a halt facing north, his gun cocked.

Later, the conscript watches curiously as the sun begins to spread along the line of the horizon. At first he cannot explain his interest to himself. Then, just as it disappears into the water, he realises than the sun has set in what he had imagined to be the east. For how many days has he been marching facing the wrong direction? For how long had he been marching up and down behind his camp instead of in front of it? In truth his orders had not stated that the threat would come from a particular direction. He had only assumed.

Now that the sun is gone he feels a little cold, sitting only in his underpants. He wraps himself in the flag that they had planted to mark the invasion of the island. It covers him adequately but the material is thinner and scratchier than he would have expected.

The conscript is composing a letter to his sweetheart. He feels he has something to say but he cannot find the right tone. He cannot even begin. My darling, he tries. Dearest. My love. Shortly he folds the unfinished letter and places it in the wooden box with all the other letters he has written to his sweetheart and the letter he has written to the author of the thriller. He picks up his gun and writes in the earth with the barrel. Sweetheart. Island. Conscript. He breaks the words down. Sweet-heart. Is-land. Con-script. He breaks them down and wonders about secret meanings. He suspects them of conspiracies. He says them aloud, again and again, until they become strange, empty. He stares at them, written in the earth, until they are no more than hieroglyphs.

The conscript sits down and tries to picture his sweetheart. He has a phrase, her heart shaped face, which he thinks is from a poem or a song. He repeats it to himself but he is no longer sure if it is appropriate and it evokes no image. Nevertheless, he continues. He licks his lips so that they are wet, as if from kissing or being kissed. In his palm the soft cloth that he uses to clean his gun covers the calluses of his hands. He holds himself delicately, awkwardly. The hand explores nervously, unsure of its skill. He does not look at the arm or the hand. He closes his eyes. He imagines it to be the hand of his sweetheart.

The conscript wakes early after a troubled night. He feels that he has dreamt many dreams but he can only recall one – dark liquid looping through the air and disappearing into the earth, over and over. He is anxious, jumpy, and when the sun comes up he believes he knows the reason why.

On the horizon, coming in and out of view, is another piece of land, another island. He sits and stares as the dawn breaks behind it, assuring himself that it is there. It is brown in colour. It appears small, but it is also far away. It is not possible to make out any features on it. Although he has not acknowledged it before now, he has the sense that its presence has been hovering at the edge of his mind, like a secret he was keeping from himself. Instantly, he knows his duty. He knows what he has to do.

He does not remember the exact moment that he loses consciousness. Is it possible to remember such a moment? It is the cold more than anything that does it. Once he was in the water the island had disappeared from view and, at times, he doubted what he had seen with his own eyes. He had tried to swim east towards where he had seen the sun rise that morning, but as the day went on he had become disorientated. He only comes to as his head scrapes against the pebbles of the beach.

The island is much the same – a little smaller perhaps, the land a little flatter, though he is not certain. He estimates the centre and then plants the flag in the earth. It is torn at one side, but he will patch it. He would like to give the island a name, for the sake of future records, but because he does not know about the existence of islands one to twenty and twenty-two and above, he feels he cannot. For the sake of clarity in his own mind, for the sake of naming it something, he names it Island 21.

His gun has survived the journey without damage. He takes it apart and cleans it. He takes his time and is thorough. Once it is reassembled he walks around the island, marking rocks at 100 yard intervals with a cross of boot polish.

Then he begins his run.

Dear John...

Uchenna Izundu

Shit, he's gone. Just like dat. Walked out, didn't say a fucking word.

Fuck.

Wot, am I meant to be surprised? I just told him I'm screwin' his best friend for God's sake. Yes you Andy, his mate, his bredrin. You, you, you. It's always bin all about fuckin' you.

Are you worth it Andy? Wot, I just dun to him? You've bin saying for time dat I need to come clean and get John out of dis cuckoo-land t'inkin' it's all safe between us.

My God, I don't even know wot to say. Well, dat's a first now, innit?

But wot am I meant to do? I can't take it no more, lyin' to him, smilin' at him when he comes up to hold me and kiss me and all I'm t'inkin' about is when I'm gonna see you. It's not right, it's just not right. And now, you know wot? Now, I'm wonderin' whether I'm off my fucking trolley mate.

John's face... Jesus... He just went blank, froze up. I thought he was gonna cry man and I'd have died of embarrassment coz I ain't ever seen him like dat. I mean wot the hell am I meant to say? I've never even seen him sniffle, yeah, not even when his mum just upped and disappeared a year ago. We've never worked out why . He said it didn't surprise him much coz she'd bin talkin' funny and she was kinda depressed ever since 'er mum had died. God, those two were close y'know. She never got over it. John had to put her on anti-depressants. Mebbe it was those dat did some kind of funny t'ing-a-ling-t'ing wiv her brain and, I dunno, got 'er to take some long walk to Dalston market and just not come back.

Andy, wot am I gonna do? I can't leave like dis. It's not right, it's not fucking right at all! But, you know wot, when I saw dat text message from Keisha, his wot-do-you-call it – "best friend who's his ex gal" - bullshit - wiv 'er all sayin' dat she "misses him today"- just wot am I meant to make of dat shit?

Of course I go ballistic. I just can't believe he was stupid enough to leave it on his phone but mebbe dat's it, mebbe it's a sign dat dis t'ing is ov-er. Oh yes. John tried sayin' dere's nuthin' going on… They're only talking… Do I Expect him to dump 'er? They were together five years, he still cares about 'er, she's his best friend… Reh, reh, fucking reh.

Do I look like I have 'fool' stamped all over my head to you? He's a first class joker! Why does he go runnin' to 'er? I'm your gal for fuck's sake. Do you remember Andy? I just bawled over the phone to you screamin' the flat down about how I'm gonna kill him; I'm havin' his baby, sortin' out his yard, and he's out and about fucking Keisha and expectin' me to grin teeth and bear it, all da way to dat tramp's bed! But then Stace has asked me why I'm carryin' on like some eediat wiv a man who's still so into his ex. Why have I gone and got preggers for him? It's stupidness of da first class order.

I remember the first time I met 'er. I bopped round to John's after work. I was feelin' mash up. My feet were killin' me from standin' around all day and my mouth hurt from grinnin' teeth at people who don't even have the slightest inklin' of respect for you, all in the name of customer service. They all think you ain't got no brains coz you're behind the till servin' them and so they carry on anyhow and are so rude. Do you know the number of times I've wanted to slap down many of dem dere and then? I've had to hold myself back yeah, squeeze my nails tight into the palm of my hand and bleed. Sheesh, I've got so many cuts there. Debs, my manager, had bin a bitch. I swear she's got issues. Some woman had seriously pissed me off talkin' to me like I'm scum off the back of 'er shoe and then had the guts to want a refund for garms dat were last season's, I tell you! It was rainin'; the fresh perm I just spent £30 on the day before might as well have bin flushed down the toilet. I was screwin'. All I wanted was for John to hold and tell me it's all gonna be sweet like chocolate.

And wot do I see?

Some Alicia Keys wannabe with zig-zagetty canerow, all cushy-tushy, legs curled up on his sofa, bussin' one of his t-shirts. She's like me, red skin, but girlfriend has some mamma-jamma thunder thighs! John was calling from the kitchen, wot does she wanna eat? He had jollof rice, shepherd's pie or was she watchin' 'er weight again and in need of a salad?

I'm like, eh-eh, wot's dis? Is it Swiss bloody family Robinson? Since when did John start offering food to gals camped out in his yard donned out in his garms? I've had to haul my arse into the kitchen and go scavengin' for mine. You know, make out like Oliver and say: 'I want some more.'

Keisha was surprised when she saw me but she quickly turned dat round - yeah, well I would too – but first she was foaming at the mouth, saying how much John spoke about me. She's been dying for all of us to get together and have supper but our schedules have never coincided. It's fabulous to meet me at last… I'm such a "poppet"… And is it raining outside? Oh darn… How annoying… I must be soooo exhausted… Just come from work? There, there… Take a seat and put up my feet…

No shit Sherlock.

Since then, I've bin on his case from day one to step from 'er, he's wiv me now - anything he says to 'er, he can bloody well say to me, y'get me? And if he can't then dat ain't right. Later! But he ain't, I don't even know whether he's tried and the more I'm on his case, yeah, the more he backs away from me.

Shit.

But I don't get it, ain't dat wot a relationship's meant to be about? Or am I wot, some kind of ready-steady-screw he comes home to jack coz he can't get none from 'er? He's fuckin' havin' his cake and eatin' it coz I know he's lyin'. He is, I know he is!

I've walked past him, chattin' nineteen-to-the-dozen to 'er, sittin' in my kitchen going on about Iraq, Bush and whether Blair will be re-elected again. I heard him mumble t'ings about savings, personal goals, setting targets and self-awareness.

In the past, I've tried to take our conversation up to the next level like he does with Keisha but he seems to lose interest real quick and then when I tell him my opinion, he asks me somethin' I ain't got the slightest clue about and then says I better start listenin' to the news then innit?

Dat pisses me right off, I don't see him clockin' the news too tough so wot makes him think he's a regular Trevor MacDonald for Christ's sake? By the time I come home, I'm shattered and I'm annoyed. Why do I wanna listen to even more depressin' stuff on TV? Dat's wot the news is like these days; all I wanna do is catch joke so I'll put on Eastenders. Dat Slater family is somet'ing else, I tell you!

But Andy, I still, I still remember when he said: 'I love the way you talk Keisha - you speak real English. It's the way you put your sentences together and all the words dat you come out with."

I just froze.

And dat's when I felt the knock on my head and my eyes burn with tears. My heart stopped tick-tock; it ain't all hickory-dock, y'get me? And I'm like, wot? Don't he think I'm clever enough to chat about dat kind of stuff? Is it coz she's at uni doing 'er law degree and I'm workin' in a shop tryin' my damndest to get into management? Our conversations are like a merry-go-round, I tell you, on the same old, same old - bills, bill, bills, wot are we doin' dis weekend, have I heard about so and so? John likes to go on about his footie, I couldn't care less. I'll moan about my cellulite, he'll tell me to stop eatin' so much then! He'll buss a joke, I'll crack up and then it's silly play-fightin' between the two of us until he moves in to kiss me.

But for dat intense second it was like I couldn't breathe. His words strangled my throat and I saw him freeze-framed, cotchin' on my couch listenin' to his Nokia as 'er voice fucked his ear. I saw 'er lips pout and 'er tongue flick in, out, shake- it- all- about. And then when John cocked his head to hold 'er voice closer, I went ape-shit.

I told him to get the fuck off the phone; ain't he got no manners? Don't she have no respect? Mans is at his gal's house so quality time means quality time. I ain't into no threesomes!

He looked at me like I just grew horns there and then and told me later. Said if I'm gonna chat to him like dat I can go to hell. Wot's wrong wiv me? Are my ears dere for decoration? All of dis is looooong. He's done the alpha and omega on their history. How can I be carrying on like dis? I need to get a grip. My jealousy ain't doin' nuthin' for nobody. I look pathetic and if dat's how I wanna stay, then he's outta here.

And I'm like, well sorry to burst your bubble mate, but I'm not dealin' wiv no part-time dad.

I'm pregnant.

Silence.

He did an exit right.

Okay, so he came back and we've tried to make it work coz John said he don't want to be the way his dad was wiv him, i.e. absent wivout leave. But dis fight, over dat text message Andy, dis one did it for me. I just couldn't take it no more about his so-called "friendship" with Keisha.

Bullshit.

I've seen him out and about wiv 'er and he don't know I'm watching - they'll be walking from Grove station, all happy-clappy, you'd think she was his woman, the way he looks at 'er so intense, so serious, like they're chatting how they're gonna get world peace. And the way he touches 'er, you know, moving 'er to the traffic light to cross the road, takin' some fluff off 'er clothes like she's some kind of diamond... Fuck 'em, fuck the two of dem!

I don't know why my conscience is playin' Jiminy Cricket wiv me sayin' I've done him wrong linkin' wiv you Andy but you know wot, I t'ink I need a lickle somet'ing somet'ing too. Damn… I knew it weren't right when you squeezed my hand and kissed my palm and touched my lips. It was all floatey-woatey. And you're all tellin' me it's okay, you're gonna be dere for me and you don't get why John is pissin' around like dis and I shouldn't get stressed, it's not good for the baby, it's not good for me…

It's just the way you said those t'ings man, all softly softly in my ear, your breath was minty and your tongue, you know, you were feelin' my hips so slow, then rubbin' my back like I'm some kind of baby. And I could smell your Jazz aftershave in the corner of your neck…mmm, you smelt so good… I just wanted to, I dunno… just mmm.

Anyhow, I can't stay here. John's gonna be coming back soon man and I don't know wot kind of mood he's gonna be in. I better start packin'.

God help me.

God's Lift is Out of Order

Karen McCarthy

Aaron is tumbling through the sky. A muddy wash of colour envelopes him like a shroud. His arms are outstretched, groping the air and he's falling, screaming my name again and again. His cries are so loud, so insistent he actually shakes me awake, out of deep dreaming sleep, the place you go to where you never remember. I sit up, struggling to see in the dark. The air is thick and wet with damp. I shiver as my pupils swell to find the light. It's morning, but it's too early for the weak winter sun. Ed thrashes around beside me, muttering and annoyed. He kicks the duvet over the edge of the thin, lumpy Futon and I snatch back at the cover, suddenly aware of the cold. Then I wake up again, out of that weird stage when you think you're awake because you're not asleep, but you're still in the dream state, and everything's slow and viscous, like you always imagined sinking in quicksand would be. I'm shouting too now, the voice in my head is the sound coming out of my mouth; Aaron's words have become my words and as he screams my name I'm screaming his and I can't stop saying it. Finally, I wake up again.

I miss the seven-forty-something out of Paddington and now it's 8.15 and we're only just pulling out of Slough, which in my mind is always pronounced like trough. I'm wearing a shoulder-padded power suit to my low paid publishing job, editing some boring computing journal out in the sticks. Late. Again. The fast train to Reading speeds by, a blast of air clipping my cheek as we lurch out of the station at two miles an hour. I stare out through the dirty glass. Grim industrial estates flicker by, gradually giving way to a more rustic vista: untidy allotments, a little field with a lone and shabby pony, bare Birch woods dotted red, white and blue with old Coke cans and plastic bags.

The train passes through Taplow, Burnham, Dorney, Bray – all apparently pretty Berkshire towns – which is strange because these aren't town names to me. They're four successive tower blocks along Adelaide Road that have mutated into a meaningless mantra inside my head – Taplow, Burnham, Dorney, Bray – always in that order. A relic from when I was six and spent whole days riding my bike round the block. But today I'm distracted from my distractions. All I can think about is Aaron.

The Prompt Corner, South End Green. The windows were always steamed up, and there were rows of formica tables, checked black and white on top, with surgical green stop clocks on the side, uniform as salt and pepper pots. The owner was Greek or Turkish – something like that, I was never sure. He was cheap though, and would put up with a gaggle of screeching pubescent girls in ripped fishnets, mini-kilts and monkey boots, drinking two teas and a hot chocolate between them for three hours. His incentive was obvious, but we never cottoned on. Eventually, he'd get sick of ogling

Sinead and Cressida – two ballerinas turned punk who went to stage school in the West End and drank cappuccinos - and tell us to spend some money or go. He didn't want us driving away his core clientele.

Old men with white hair and black wrinkles and a few tweedie academics would sit there all day sipping endless coffees, smoking Gitanes and playing chess against the clock. On Saturday afternoons Aaron would sit among them, ignoring us on the other side of the room. At fourteen he was a nationally ranked player; but as he confided one night while we were lying on the floor of my bedroom, pretending not to notice our legs were touching and flicking through X-Men comics: he always tried to keep his grading low for competitions. I couldn't understand for ages; my motto was if you've got it flaunt it. He walked me through the whole concept slowly until the penny finally dropped. You win more money that way.

That day he only broke even, so we all bunked in round the back to see The Exorcist at the Hampstead Classic on a late night. About eight of us sat in the back row, feet on seats, munching our way through giant size cartons of popcorn, smoking Bensons and calling each other cunts. All the girls shrieked at the bit with the projectile vomiting and grabbed on to the boys.

'Your mother sucks cocks in hell!' we growled, over and over, while attempting 360° head swivels as we trooped out of the cinema at half one in the morning. I did it too, but only half-heartedly: one because I didn't know anything about sucking cocks which was embarrassing, and two because I was terrified of becoming possessed like the girl in the film.

Aaron and I weren't like real Hampstead kids who lived next door to titled architects and TV personalities. We had to get the North London Line home to Kilburn, or walk back past the cemetery. I had an evil step-dad and he had the wicked witch of the north, south, east and west running the show at his place. His real mum was in a loony bin up north somewhere, but we never really talked about that. He was more clever than me: he could read music, write poetry, play chess, piano, basketball. They all listened to Radio 3 at his house, and he could do maths.

On the way back to mine we detoured via the hospital because it had a hot chocolate machine and, as usual, I was dying to do a wee. We were fidgeting in the foyer by the lifts for ages before we realised they weren't working.

'Look at that – God's lift is out of order.' The sign actually read, "Goods lift is out of order." 'We'll never get to heaven then,' I laugh, enjoying the brief moment of my mistake.

'Or the toilets,' he countered, suddenly making a face and staggering towards me with a zombie flesh eater look. 'This is the one that goes straight up to the LOCKED WARD.'

I swiped at him, in that 'girl hits boy but doesn't really mean it' way and tried to look serious. After all, I've still got to go to the loo on my own.

Back in the home counties, I arrive half an hour late for work and am immediately confronted by Ivy, who calls out 'Morning' as loud as she possibly can.

'Trouble with the trains?' Eileen asks, looking at her watch. I sweep off to the kitchen to fetch a tea and when I return Ivy is standing at my desk.

'You see, it's not consistent,' she waves the offending article at me. 'Look, on page 34 you've got COBOL in small caps and here it's upper and lower case.'

Eileen and Ivy spend their days typing faster than I can edit and complaining about my consistency – or lack of it. I console myself with the thought that it must be tough having me as their boss: I'm about fifty years younger than they are and as yet I haven't seen any other black people in the whole town - never mind our office.

Eileen stares over at me, pushes her low-slung Deidre Barlow glasses up to the bridge of her nose and smiles.

'So, are you going back for Christmas then?'

'Back ?' I ask, knowing full well where this one's heading.

'Well, it is Jamaica isn't it?' Ivy doesn't bother with the smile.

I spend lunchtime scouring The Bookseller for jobs.

Two weeks pass and it's Christmas Eve before I know it. Ed's away in Wales with his family and I'm getting ready for Dano's birthday party, alone. As usual I'm wandering around aimlessly, rummaging through pyramids of clothes; conjuring mess like a magician pulling rabbits from a hat. I start shuffling through an irrelevant pile of papers and turn up an antique card covered in inky violets. It had arrived on Valentine's Day – anonymous. Even though I had recognised the writing, I couldn't quite believe it was from Aaron.

But things were different now: the Prompt Corner was a Perfect Pizza, and I saw more of Aaron's older brother who used to come round, chop up vast lines of dodgy sulphate, then disappear mysteriously to the bathroom for twenty minutes. The last time I'd seen Aaron he was fat with Largactil or 'liquid cosh' – the stuff they pumped people full of in prison to keep them quiet. He sat round the kitchen table for what seemed like days. He could communicate with Marilyn Monroe. The conductor of the orchestra he played violin in had put a black magic hex on him. He knew what had really happened with the Kennedys. I grimaced. So, the rumours were true: Aaron Gold had taken too much acid and lost the plot.

I arrive at Dano's party. It's in one of those big, white houses with tall, tall ceilings in Belsize Park. The bass is booming out Lee Perry and the front room is heaving with people so the whole floor is bouncing up and down in time to the music and Dano's freaking out because it's his parent's house and he's worried it's literally going to fall down. I make my way to the kitchen, through a hallway lined with people who couldn't stand me at school and spot Kevin McConnell in a black trilby, holding court by the fridge. I wave and wade through the crowd.

Before I can ask, he asks, 'Have you heard about Aaron?'

'What?' Visions of strait jackets, needles and looming Nurse Ratchetts run through my mind. 'Has his dad had him committed again?'

Kevin looks at me, and pauses for a second, 'He jumped out Burnham. Out of my brother Kieran's flat. Out the window. Didn't you know?' I keep staring, and he finishes his sentence. 'The 22nd floor.'

I can't move. All I can think about is the last time we spoke. It was early days for me and Ed and we were so in love we could hardly walk straight. Ed's there with my flatmate and her boyfriend and we're all pissing around, having a laugh. The phone rang. It was him. I'd told them all the stories, they knew about the card. He was playing jazz piano at Dingwalls. Did I want to come? But I'm barely listening and suddenly I'm barking strange messages down the phone, mum should never have given you this number and don't call here again. I could hear this party in the background and his voice getting smaller and smaller and I wanted to tell him I was sorry, that I didn't mean it, that I missed him. But everybody was listening, so I didn't. I put the phone down instead.

A thin blond girl trips over my foot and spills red wine on me without apologising.

Kevin McConnell finally realises that I didn't know.

'When?' It's all I can say, even though I already know the answer.

I stick my head out the window, feel the cold air bite against my skin and shut my eyes.

Aaron is tumbling through the sky. A muddy wash of colour envelopes him like a shroud. His arms are outstretched, groping the air ahead of him and he's falling, screaming my name, again and again.

I am more awake than I have ever been. This is not a dream.

Coming Of Age

Niall Griffiths

See, he's not my proper son, not by blood, like, but I adter take him on as family when I married his mother, didn't I? Ad no choice in the matter. I mean yeh can tell he's not one of mine just by looking at him; more meat on a jockey's whip. A strong fart'd blow him away. No way he's gunna have any blood of mine in his veins, is there? But his mum, she likes her bit of rough, like, and I'm partial to a blonde brewstered divorcee with tits all bought n paid for like a pair of friggin watermelons, so I adter take her boy on when I married her, didn't I? Don't know who his father was; some penpusher, friggin accountant or somet, never done a day's real work in his life. Dodgy genes, like, knowmean? But, y'know, he's part of the family now whether I fuckin like it or not and he turned 18 last week an I asked him what he wanted for a prezzie and djer know what he said? A buke. A fuckin buke! For his 18th! Gunner spend the day he becomes a man fuckin reading! Fucks to that, man. Bollox. So c'med, said I, I'll take yeh for yer first pint, yer first legal bevvy as a man. Told the missis I was taking him to the winebar, just a quiet couple like, an she was happy. Half way down a bottle of gin and twenty friggin Prozac inside her, course the daft bint was happy.

An the little get didn't wanna go but I wasn't gunna take no for an answer. He said

I'm not going I said ye fuckin are. Tradition, this, I said; you become part of my fuckin family and you'll take part in its traditions. I did this with my old man on my 18th, and he did it with his. Fuckin heritage, lad, I said. He says that he doesn't drink. I told him every lad of mine drinks, fuckin stepson just or no. Besides, place I was gunna take him to, probly best off if he didn't drink. Keep the lead in his pencil, like, knowmean?

So yeh, I takes him down the Dock Road, to the Crown. Thursday Night Special, wannit? We goes in an all the lads're already there, Willy an his brothers, Bob Thompson, all just clocked off an already friggin steamboats the lot of them, not even seven o' clock. The boy's gone all shy an fuckin timid like but I plonks him down an Willy puts his arm round him an starts singin Happy Birthday loud in his friggin ear like an I goes up to the bar an gets two pints an a double vodders, slips the vodders into the pint I give the boy. He sips at it an goes fuckin green, looks like he's just about to friggin honk up all over the table. Honest to God, there's no blood of mine in him, no fuckin way. Pure embarrassing if there was, tellin yeh.

The place is fuckin chocka, all blokes like with it bein a Thursday, dead hot n sweaty, y'know the way it gets in there. Bouncer's already havin a hard time tryna keep this fuckin shower under control like an the first girl hasn't even come on stage yet. Never seen it that packed. The boy, well, he's like a fuckin rabbit in headlights, inny? He's never seen anything like it before in his life, knowmean? Should be enjoyin himself like but he looks like he's gunna up an leg it any fuckin minute. Felt like tellin him that becomin a man ain't bleedin easy, it's not meant to be just fun; it's somet you've gorra, what, fuckin endure. Happens to us all. Get used to it lad, face it fuckin head-on an be brave I wanted to say but the noise is so loud yeh can't speak like it fuckin always is on a Thursday an anyways Willy's still holdin the boy, singin in his ear. He's gone red as a beetroot, the boy. Square peg in round hole. But fair play to him he manages to finish his glass an Bob goes up to get him another. I tip ahl Bob the wink as he passes so that he'll know to spike it an he gives us a grin an a nod. Good lad, Bob. Knows the score, that man; see, same thing happened to him on his 18th, didn't it? It's what happens to all the bucks round here when they come of age, like; their old man takes em down the Crown. First legal night on the piss, first sniff of fanny. Heritage, lad, innit? Pure heritage. Tradition. Simple as. An where the fuck would we be without it, eh?

The lad must've had five, six pints an several neat vodkas unbeknownst to him like by the time the first girl comes on. That dark girl, Melody she calls herself altho her real name's fuckin Eileen or somet. Bold girl, like. Not fuckin shy, knowmean? An she's down to her knickers, red crotchless numbers like, doin the splits at the front of the stage so close ye could friggin smell it an the lad's eyes, they're on fuckin stalks man, tellin yiz. Never seen anythin like ar Melody in his life. Looked like he was about to fuckin blub or somet to be honest an then all the lads start pointin at him an chantin

18! 18! 18! over n over again an the girl, that Melody one, she comes straight over to him through the crowd, hands all fuckin over her like an she sits down on his knee an rubs her tits in his face y'know the way they do, an then she just ups an fuckin drags the poor lad on stage. Drags him by the hand an she's got some strength that girl; poor bastard's got no choice but to follow her up, has he? I mean her arms're twice the size of his. Crowd's goin nuts like an he's up there shakin like a fuckin leaf. Almost started to feel sorry for him but Jeez he's 18, he's a man; gorra learn to behave like one, hasn't he? This kinda thing hurts, sometimes; he's gorra learn that. It ain't all easy, becomin a man. I mean, look at me; three wives in ten years, no fuckin picnic, that, lad. Divorce is a messy fuckin business, no lie. You stop bein a kid an things start gettin friggin complicated, don't they? Nowt easy in this world. Fuck no. Just somethin you've gorra learn. Just gorra have someone to help ye through it, like.

So she took his kex down. Just unzipped em an let them drop with his undies n all an there he is, tremblin like, bollocko, swayin either with terror or the bevvy or both like, this friggin shrivelled worm-thing between his legs, on show for all to see. Awful. Fuckin awful. An that Melody, she takes his knob an points it out at the audience an the crowd went even crazier, pissin themselves laughin, an the lad starts cryin but he's just standin there, kex round his ankles like, fuckin humiliatin for the boy. Everyone's laughin at him an Melody tips him on his back on the floor with his feet facing the crowd like an she gets on top of him an tries to shag him, I mean as I say she's not fuckin shy that one, but Jeez. . . like tryna shove a marshmallow in a fuckin parkin meter. Pure fuckin embarassin it was. Bob an Willy an the rest of the lads, they're in fuckin fits an I'm standin up, shoutin at the boy to fuckin give her one for me like but nowt's happenin. Honest to God, hung like a Chinese mouse, him. Fuckin mortifyin, it was. An I weren't gunna be showed up like that was I so I says fuck this an gets up on the stage meself, Melody's squatting like with her back to the audience, can't see me, an I gets into position behind her. Bouncer comes steamin over but he can't get through the crush, an anyway I'm in the girl up to the friggin plums in a second. Gorra show the boy how to do it, like, haven't I? Course I have. Retain some self-respect, like, innit? Pure fuckin embarrassin, that. Stepson or no, he's associated with me, it was me who took him there. Makin me look a knob'ed, that. Melody's now leanin forward on her hands like, hands an knees, straddlin the lad, an I'm givin it to her so friggin hard that I've pushed her forward an I only realize too late like that we're both positioned over the boy's face; I mean he's still flat on his back on the deck, blubbin away like a ponce. No blood of mine in that boy, honest to God. But aye, he's still in that position when I pull out so I couldn't help where I friggin bloshed, could I? I couldn't help where it went. Taught the softarse a lesson, anyway, didn't it? If yer knocked over, get back up on yer feet. Fuckin end of lesson. Simple as. An if yeh can't gerrit up yeh gerrout of there quickquick. Got things to learn, that boy, no fuckin lie.

So yeh, that was me; I did me thing then gave it toes. Too fuckin embarrassed to hang around, everyone there thinkin he was me blood relative, like. Mortified I was. Went off on a bender for a couple of days, gets home hungover to shite like and there She is, going on, what have I done to her son, in a terrible state, won't come out of his room, locked himself in, all this shite. About a week ago this was an I haven't seen the lad since. Not sure I want to, either, just yet, to be honest with yiz; I mean, right fuckin embarrassin episode that was. No son of mine who can't gerrit up. Try an show someone a bit of heritage, get them involved like, try an include them in yer family's history an what happens? See what yer get? A loader friggin grief, that's what. Everyone laughin at yer on the shopfloor. Tellin yeh; next birthday, if we're both still around like, he'll get his friggin buke. Wish I'd never bothered now, to be honest. Fuckin farce, that's what it was. Just embarrassin.

Biographies

SHARON JENNINGS

A Social Care Consultant and lecturer, Sharon has published articles and books on black mental health and complementary therapies, but she has also been writing poetry and short stories for several years. Her stories appear in the Kin Anthology of Black and Asian writing and she is working on a historical novel based in England where she has lived and worked for almost 30 years having migrated from the US.

RAJEEV BALASUBRAMANYAM

Rajeev's first novel In Beautiful Disguises, published by Bloomsbury in 2000 when the author was just 25. It won the Betty Task Award and was nominated for the Guardian Fiction Prize. His short story The Dreamer won an Ian St. James Short Story Award. His second novel, in progress, is based on this short story. Born in Lancaster, he splits his time between London and Berlin. Rajeev is Features Editor for Sable magazine.

LIAM GALLIMORE-WELLS

London-born writer and internationally renowned spoken word recording artist, Liam Gallimore-Wells supported Linton Kwesi Johnson at the 2002 Bristol International Poetry Festival and his short fiction was first showcased on the 2001 ExCommunicate Literary Tour. His short stories have been published in iQ and Decode magazine and he has collaborated with French rock band Toxic Twins. Liam has just completed a tour of China and the Far East and his debut EP with electronica artist Monstatruk will be released on Underconstruction Records later this year. He is currently working on his first novel, Dead Air.

MATT THORNE

Still only twenty-nine, Matt Thorne's career to date is remarkable. His first novel Tourist, a tale of betrayals, emotional scars and unorthodox sexual relationships in the seedy seaside town of Weston, was long-listed for the Guardian Fiction Prize. His second novel Eight Minutes Idle won a 1999 Encore Award and his third Dreaming Of Strangers, is currently being adapted for film by director Steve Barron. Matt's other novels are Pictures of You, Child Star, and Cherry, which is being published by Weidenfeld and Nicolson in September this year. Matt has also edited a collection of short stories along with Nicholas Blincoe entitled All Hail The New Puritans and recently published his first children's book Greengrove Castle (Faber).

SALENA GODDEN

Lead singer of ska-punk trio SaltPervert, Saleena Godden is also a poet, broadcaster & performer. Her work has appeared in the two most recent Coldcut albums Let us Play and Let us Replay (Ninja Tune) and she is currently writing lyrics/poetry for their new album out later this year. As well as being featured in the underground press, Godden has been published in Penguin's IC3 & Serpents Tail's Oral anthologies. She is also the muse for new French fashion label Princess Prostitute Idiot. Last year Saliva featured on BBC Radio 4's new spoken word series 'Bespoken Word' and co-presented Channel 4's late night discussion series HEAVY TV. She is currently writing a documentary, Seaside Rocks for Channel 4's MADE IN BRITAIN series, which she will also present.

BARBARA GRAHAM

Barbara Graham is a British born Jamaican living in East London with her family. Her writing has grown out of journaling after the death of her father. Her first short story Next of Kin was published in the Kin Anthology edited by Karen McCarthy. She is currently studying English part time at the University of North London and is working on making writing her significant other occupation.

SHIROMI PINTO

Shiromi Pinto is a writer and editor based in North London. Her short story, Trussed, appears in Kin, an anthology of women's writing (Serpent's Tail). Kolambe, a travel memoir, is published in the autumn 2001 issue of the Toronto Review of Contemporary Writing Abroad and on opendemocracy.net, alongside South Beach – another short story. Her first short story, Bulat Kisses, appeared in Notes Across the Aisle (Thistledown Press, Saskatchewan) and was awarded second prize in the publisher's 1995 short story competition.

ABBY AJAYI

Abby Ajayi was born in London, in 1979, to Nigerian parents. She grew up in Lagos and London and still lives in North London. She works as a Script Editor for the BBC and writes short stories and short films. She also has several unfinished novels. Abby is currently writing a screenplay - a thriller based in London.

NII AYIKWEI PARKES

Born in England and raised in Ghana, Nii Parkes is an internationally-respected performance poet and writer. A UK Poetry Slam champion and veteran of several poetry festivals, throughout the world and has appeared on major stages such as the NuYorican Poets Café, the Royal Festival Hall and Glastonbury Festival. Nii's work has been published in several magazines and journals including SABLE Literary Magazine, Poetry News, x magazine, and Peace Poems (Crocus Press). His recently completed first novel, The Cost of Red Eyes won a 2003 Arts Council award.

DZIFA BENSON

Dzifa Benson was born in London but spent her formative years in Africa until she returned to the UK to attend university at the age of 17. She cites her heritage as Ghanaian, "but I am very much a Londoner". Dzifa is an established music journalist and has contributed to the Guardian, Evening Standard and Trace magazine among others. As well as writing a radio play, a novel and penning poetry on a daily basis, she is currently working with a with a film company on a documentary about African music.

STEVE PORTER

Steve Porter has had seven short stories published over the years, and has the usual three unpublished novels under the bed, one of which enabled him to get an MA in Writing from Sheffield-Hallam University. He runs a literature development project in West London and in his spare time, of which there isn't much, he continues towards his dream of getting a novel published. He lives in Harlesden with a very patient girlfriend.

MARTIN OUVRY

Martin was born in Sussex and lives in west London. After working as a musician in Europe and America, he gained a First in English at the University of East Anglia, took the MA course in Creative Writing, and was awarded the UEA Alumni Association Prize for Fiction. He is at work on a novel, with the support of a grant from the Arts Council England.

TOM LEE

Tom Lee lives in London where he is working on a novel. His stories have appeared in the Dublin Review and in Zembla.

UCHENNA IZUNDU

Uchenna Izundu was born in Nigeria and spent her early childhood in Scotland. She has been writing stories from an early age. Uchenna is an energy journalist, specialising in the news and analysis of international geo-politics and commercial developments of global gas projects. She is a board member of Aspire, a support organisation for black media professionals that aims to connect potential black journalists with those already working within the industry. Her work has been broadcast on the BBC World Service and has appeared in The Guardian, New Nation, Asian Times, African Times and darkerthanblue.com. Her creative writing has been published in Penguin's IC3 and Sable Literary magazine.

NIALL GRIFFITHS

Niall Griffiths was born in Liverpool in 1966 and now lives in Aberystwyth. Both towns have a strong hold on his imagination. He burst on to the literary scene in 2000 with Grits (Jonathan Cape), a ferocious novel narrated through a revolving series of vernacular voices, which is currently being adapted for television. Sheepshagger (Jonathan Cape) followed in 2001, and in many ways, was a sharpening of focus, confirming Griffiths's reputation as a serious novelist of striking originality. His third novel, Kelly and Victor (Jonathan Cape) appeared in 2002, and is being turned into a feature film. Stump, (Jonathan Cape, 2003), traces a trajectory of violent retribution between Liverpool and Aberystwyth, following two shell-suited gangsters on their journey from Merseyside to the seaside town to settle a score. This is also being filmed. Griffiths's work has been translated into several languages and he has read his work at various festivals in various countries. His latest novel, Wreckage, will appear in 2005.

COURTTIA NEWLAND (editor)

When Courttia Newland published his first novel The Scholar aged 23, he immediately captivated the media as one of the few black British writers who accurately portrayed teenage life in London's inner cities. The Scholar quickly became a bestseller and is currently being made into a film. His second novel Society Within, set on the same fictional Greenside Estate in West London, was published in 2002. His third book Snakeskin, although set in the same world, is a detective novel. Courttia has a solid reputation in theatre; his play Mother's Day, premiered at the Lyric Studio in Hammersmith, and B is for Black sold out its three week run at the Oval House Theatre; and has contributed to many short story volumes including Disco 2000, Afrobeat and the Time Out Book of London Short Stories. Along with Kadija George, he edited IC3, a collection of stories and poetry reflecting the first, second and third generations of British black writing. He is writer in residence at the London College of Communication, and runs a weekly creative writer's workshop in Shepherd's Bush Library, West London.